Geoff Nelder

Book Two
of
The Flying Crooked
Series

FALLING UP

If you thought *SUPPOSE WE* was surreal, a bit odd, yet recapturing the magic and passion of space exploration, just wait till you read *FALLING UP!*

- Geoff Nelder

FALLING UP
Paperback version

ISBN: 978-0-9975549-4-6

Published in the USA by LL-Publications 2019
www.ll-publications.com
PO Box 542
Bedford
Texas 76095

Edited by Billye Johnson
Book layout and typesetting by jimandzetta.com
Cover design by jimandzetta.com

GEOFF NELDER'S BOOKS

Humorous thriller *ESCAPING REALITY.*

Award-winning science fiction mystery with a hot-blooded heroine, *EXIT, PURSUED BY A BEE.*

Another thriller, *HOT AIR*, received an Award d'Or from an Arts Academy in the Netherlands.

A science fiction trilogy, *ARIA* with an original premise is published by LL-Publications. It won the P&E readers poll in 2012

Historical fantasy, *XAGHRA'S REVENGE* is set in the Maltese islands and based on a true mass abduction of the people of Gozo in 1551.

INCREMENTAL is a collection of 25 of Geoff Nelder's more surreal short stories.

SUPPOSE WE is book one of the Flying Crooked series.

Summary of *Suppose We:* book one of the *Flying Crooked* series.

Suppose We leaves Earth five-hundred years from now as one of several SpaceWeb exploration ships seeking habitable planets. There's a crew of four humans and its AI. The human crew are put into hibernation for a thousand years while the ship approaches the Kepler-20 planetary system. Their mission is more complex than they think because SpaceWeb has installed a tiny package of human genomes, known only to the ship's AI to use when appropriate to colonise a planet. Taking large numbers of humans or their embryos is so 21st century thinking whereas genomes can be packed in a small pocket. Unfortunately, the hibernation meds disrupt the mind of the commander, Penn, which makes him more aggressive and he destroys a Jupiter-size sphere he thought was about to attack *Suppose We.* The AI also has a breakdown in its own way, but that's another story. No, it's part of this story as you'll see.

The selected planet, Kepler-20h is not as uninhabited as believed, but it might as well be because the highly evolved natives completely ignore the humans who desperately need help after they crash-land.

Kepler-20h has an unEarthlike ecosystem, being without predators. However, a mutated, aggressive bacteria has plagued organic and inorganics alike giving the *Suppose We* crew an opportunity to offer a solution. The rogue bacteria has been modified to contain prion protein molecules with a human genome (H.NewKep). The prion teaches the old bacteria how to stack and lock, spreading rapidly through the planet. Humans? Yes, but not as you know them, at least for a thousand generations and even then they could be a cross between a terrapin and moss, but with an appreciation for jazz.

As the four humans: Commander Penn with engineer Delta; Science officer Gaston and navigator Em start to enjoy their new planet with the former pair repairing *Suppose We* and the latter exploring, a threat approaches the Kepler system. Spheres made of spinning wire wool – a galactic lawnmower out to seek revenge for the stolen oxygen from their planets.

Quotes about SUPPOSE WE, the first in the Crooked Flight series, and FALLING UP, book two.

David Leaper:

This is a cracking story, showing lots of imagination. Sci-Fi fans will not be disappointed by this latest effort by Geoff Nelder. Looking forward to the next book in The Flying Crooked series.

Mark Iles:

I've read all of Geoff Nelder's work, found them all superbly written and SUPPOSE WE is no exception. What a fabulous read, can't believe it was only delivered this morning and I've read it already! Geoff's world building is exemplary, the character conflict brilliant, and there's a real sense of other worldiness with the Kep. With the senses all covered you find yourself really invested in the tale. Loved 'Papillon', naming the 'butterfly' that really made me smile.

Martin Lamberti:

Just as the Cabbage White's flight is unpredictable, so the quirky beginnings of Suppose We in Geoff's newest release. I'm looking forward to the continuation of the crooked flights of the series that we suppose we CAN. (As in CANDID)

Rosie Oliver author and aeronautical engineer:

Falling Up has many forms of reality interlaced into this space opera - actual reality, surreality, the virtual reality of data, and a type of reality Geoff has invented that is all too possible in science.

Dr Jacques Coulardou:

Imagination, when compared to life, is so absurd that it becomes fascinating, mesmerizing and even hypnotizing. And Geoff Nelder really puts the smallest dishes imaginable into the biggest ones till the latter are overflowingly full.

Dr Bob Smith, psychologist:

The best thing about reading speculative fiction is the creative imagination of someone else, who thinks up things (even) I haven't. If the writing is good, I join into the author's reality-construction while reading. Then, afterward, the new concepts challenge me. I muse over "what if" considerations, and perhaps my view of the possible is enlarged.

This is why I enjoy Geoff Nelder's writing. He and I think very differently. At first, some of his concepts strike me as bizarre -- then they grow on me. (Please don't take that literally.)

His latest, a story named after the spaceship, "Suppose We," is just like that. The narrator, small, slight but bouncy Frenchman Gaston, is delightful. The four humans in the story have very real, contrasting personalities, leading to some fun and games, but most enjoyable is a character who names itself CAN, and then has endless fun punning on the name.

Peter Wilhelmsen, fantasy writer

- *One of the things I love most about Falling Up (and Suppose We), is that it never stops being curious. The characters, action and drama on the mind-boggling planet our humans are stranded on makes it one of the most original sci-fi stories I've read in a long while.*
- *The only possible explanation on how the world and the aliens feel so real despite their unreal appearance is that the author himself must have visited Kepler-20h at some point.*

- *If there's one thing I've learnt while reading Falling Up, it's that you never stop fighting no matter how hostile the environment is. Oh, and if your leader is a trigger-happy, impulsive man-child you do your best to keep him on a short leash when dealing with the natives.*
- *Falling Up is an awesome ride. The characters jump out of their pages and their personalities really shine through.*

Magdalena Ball of the Compulsive Reader review site:

There's always an element of action, a hint of steamy romance, and Nelder's trademark twist."

Acknowledgements

Once again, I have enjoyed the combined literary wisdom of the Orbiter 7 novel critique group of the British Science Fiction Association. In particular, Mark Iles, Rosie Oliver, Dr David Allan, Dunstan Power, Chris Rimell, Peter Wilhelmsen and the overall Orbiter coordinator, Terry Jackman. They nit-picked, lacerated and improved my manuscript no end. Even so, any faults are all down to my own wackiness.

My wife for putting up with looking at my back while I write. The Chester Science Fiction Book Group, who kindly do not discuss my stories while I'm in the room.

International online game players like David Leaper, Steven Whitener, Professor Drucilla Ronchen, Marianne Boehlert, Mary Frances, Kerry Kaufman, Rita and John Marchant and international entertainer, Martin Lamberti, have all bought my works and boosted my flagging ego.

I have social media friends, who actively encourage my writing. It would take over 50 pages to mention them all but special thanks to Cameron MacDonald Black – Scottish poet (Still Barking at Dogs) and Les Floyd @LesFloyd in Carlisle.

I also acknowledge Jim and Zetta Brown of LL-Publications and the keen eye of their editor, Billye Johnson, for their support and encouragement.

Dedication

Dedicated to Gaynor, my understanding wife, son Rob, daughter Eleanor, and their marvellous families.

Foreword & Travellers' Notes

All the characters in this tale are fictional although they have a past life in book one, *SUPPOSE WE*.

Readers will find the Kepler 20 system really exists although the Kepler-20h planet and the nearby alien artificial intelligence base have yet to be spotted. If you point your fingers between Cygnus and Lyra, they'll be in the right direction for the location of this story.

I am passionate about space exploration stories. Earth is too limited for my runaway imagination. Luckily, there are hundreds of science fiction authors with strange planets in their heads for me to explore. This book realises and releases a lifelong urge to paint my own vision of what a strange, yet habitable planet might be like and how we might react to alien encounters. I spurn the traditional shoot-em-up military SF in this series although enemies attack and retaliated against but in unusual ways. I enjoy breaking tropes.

Coming soon...

The third book in the Crooked Flight series is ***Kepler's Son***. If readers thought Suppose We bore original touches and strangeness then found Falling Up continued in the same vein only more surreal, just wait for Kepler's Son. The humans, the native keps and hybrid creatures that might have inherited the best of both, the worst of both. The reader goes back into space, but not as they know it.

FALLING UP

Observation voice playback in 4, 3, 2, 1!

'From beyond the system and out of the blackness, the scopes picked up a flash of purple. A deadly bladed orb entered the outer Kepler20 system. As if it was a gigantic wire wool ball hurtling through space, it was superb at dicing what it considered to be an enemy. In this case Kep20-m, the most outer wanderer of this system, sparsely populated, a lonely soul, and smaller than Earth's Moon. It was the first victim to be diced. Imagine a Jupiter-sized ball apparently composed of rotating micro razor-sharp filaments. The forlorn planet initially stayed as a sphere after the artefact sliced through it. The molten core hardly noticed the incursion as liquid nickel reformed. However, the mantle and crust waited a few moments before separating like a slow explosion. We think the wire wool induced like-charges, which then repelled each other. One minute, a deluded observer would see the planet as a whole sphere, but as seconds dragged on, it puffed apart into space. Gravity would eventually bring the particles back together, rearranged. Deranged. Only the molten core remained intact. An angry red fist shaking at the outrage as it heads for us.'

Recorded by Navigator Em using the Keps orbiting observatory g236

CHAPTER ONE

Her run through the abandoned mine left Em exhausted. Her muscles wondered when she was going to rest, as did her brain. Miners on Earth usually dug straight adit tunnels into a mountain, but here on Kepler-20h the snakelike meanders made it hard to run in the musty darkness. She'd tripped, twice, obliging Penn to hurl himself against the rough wall to avoid barging into her.

"Em, use your headtorch. I can hear the bastards catching up."

Tears filled her eyes. They'd been running all day through an alien jungle then into this abandoned mine – evidenced by rusted machinery with gears, cogs, and broken pipes, not unlike machines on Earth. Their discovery of eviscerated animal remains freaked them both out and when they sighted hairy quadrupeds, they'd run. The thought of them tearing apart and eating the gentle herbivores of this planet sent shivers through her. She'd tried to navigate a course back to the Northern Expedition Base, but the undergrowth and their need to escape terrifying pursuers led to this mine. She needed to inform Gaston and Delta that their assumption of zero predators on this planet might have been unfounded, although...

She tapped into their AI. "CAN, did you see our footage of the creatures chasing us?"

Her ear buzzed with the weak signal, 'Busy.'

"CAN, they might be an advance party from those approaching aliens with ships looking like wire wool. Please review our images and scan the area."

'Go away, Navigator Em Farrer. It is on the list. I am involved with the Keps attempting to communicate with said invaders. Out.'

Annoyed at their AI's rudeness, she took a moment to return to her normal tough persona, put out a hand to steady herself and wished she hadn't. Even before she put her now sticky hand to her nose she smelt something no human was supposed to experience: a cross between rotting fruit and a Keplerian slug slime.

She scrunched up her nostrils. "What did they mine in here? Molluscs?"

Penn pushed his short but muscular body past her. "Coming up fast."

"Leave me, why don't you? Ah, you've left a calling card, yes?" She accelerated to catch him. There he went, legs going like egg-beaters. The flashes from her light periodically lit up his green SpaceWeb fatigues. She wore the same colour but set off with her long blond braids that now whipped her backpack.

They rounded a bend to be blinded by sunlight. Penn skidded to a halt just in time to stagger as she fell into him.

"Why did you stop? Oops." She saw how they'd emerged at a semi-circular exit, but as if it had been drilled half way up a cliff. "This is crazy, we're hundreds of metres up!"

Em slumped on the cool stone floor and permitted herself a brief respite. Her thoughts retreated back a couple of days. They'd swapped partners and missions for a change of pace and scenery just before regrouping next week for a meeting with the Keps about the incoming alien craft.

Her Gaston was now up to his elbows in an ancient Kep vehicle assembly with Delta. At the same abandoned settlement, which was apparently half a million years old, Penn and Em set up a Northern exploration base. It was surrounded by steppe—mostly flat purple grasslands with gentle rivers, and occasional woodland in depressions.

⊙X⊙

"This is my cup of tea," Em had said, as she unwisely chewed on a stem of lilac grass.

"It's okay, I guess," Penn said. "But it's just an endless plain. What do you get out of it?"

She laughed, partly at his crass-tease and at a green mouse-like creature darting across their path. A stump of a tail and a red berry in one hand. It stopped, looked at them in astonishment and ran off between the metre-high grasses. "I love the stark beauty of the ground and the enormous sky."

Penn stamped a foot crushing what might have passed for a beetroot-stained barley. "Too busy to admire the fucking sky. I'm sick of these cursed stalks curling round my ankles trying to trip me up. Sure they're not man-eating?"

She too had to be careful, but it was no different from avoiding being tripped in an English meadow. "Perhaps we should've agreed to take a hover. Hey, see what I see?"

Penn crunched to a halt, now also chewing on a stalk, probably wishing it was beef jerky. Em smiled at the sight of it disappearing into his red facial hair. "What? That low greenish cloud?"

"Ah, I thought you'd think it was a mirage as I did. Love those optical phenomena in the desert."

Em remembered a reference to seeing them in the Mediterranean. "Suppose it could be a Fata Morgana. Optical phenomena appearing to be floating cities, cliffs or forests. Hehe, even with ancient spirits taking us to their homes. However, it looks too smooth even for a lenticular cloud. Hang on, I'll use the scope. I see rectilinear and spherical shapes inside it. Could be teeth in a giant, grinning mouth. What d'you see?"

Penn grinned while stroking his out-of-control red beard. "Me too. A city. Wonderful. Let's head over there. Can't be more than five K."

She had to put away the scope in case she tripped as they hiked, but beneath the apparition was the usual blurred and wavering imagery in the hot air. It really could be a Fata Morgana mirage.

Like the real Russian Steppe, the landscape was more undulating than flat with areas of difficulty such as bogs and thorny scrubland. Several long zigzags later, they climbed a low hill and stopped to enjoy a snack. The elongated mouth shape was still up in the sky, closer but hardly clearer. Its pearlescent colours would render it nearly invisible in some light conditions.

Beans fell out of Penn's tortilla-like wrap as he squeezed too hard. "That's never a mirage, girl."

Em had sat on a white quartzite boulder to brew a kind of tea with a self-heating pot. "I'm inclined to agree. It's a floating ... airship?"

"Maybe, though it'd be a fucking huge one. Alert! Something coming up behind us. Pass me the scope."

Damn, just as her tea made with what might be raspberry leaves was ready, filling her nostrils with a hot fruity aroma. She stood only to be pulled down again. She unhooked the scope from around her neck, and blew like crazy on the steaming tea.

"Monkeys, apes, whatever. Using all four limbs. Ungainly but heading for us. There's woodland a kilometre southwest. You go first, I'll slow 'em down."

She unbent up just enough to see their movement through the wavy grasses. "No engagement. Remember?"

"Yeah. I was outvoted but I won't fire on them, just ignite the grass in front of the bastards."

"They might just want some tea and a chat?" Though she doubted it.

"Get going, you peace freak." So, she did. Through the woods, into this cave that turned out to be a kind of mine tunnel and now at this no-easy-escape exit.

"Actually, I'm getting used to this damn planet," Penn grumbled. "Designed by Salvador Dali after one too many riojas. Wait. They should've reached my surprise."

He checked his wrist SmartPad. "Ugh, they must've sensed the sensor."

She looked back into the gloom. "We underestimated them."

Penn tapped at his device. "At least I can bring down the roof. Best to get outside, not much of a ledge. Try to merge into the cliff."

The rumbling travelled right through her, followed by the cliff-face shaking. She unplugged her fingers out of her ears and dug them into the white rock. She looked over at Penn doing the same thing while voicing 'sorry'.

Her fingers proved to be poor pitons once the outblast blew out of the mine, taking her with it. Her stomach griped and icy fingers ran up her spine when she found herself momentarily suspended a few metres from the entrance, Lord knows how high off the ground and surrounded by an assortment of white and grey stones. She couldn't see Penn, but in order to call his name, she first had to stop screaming.

Perhaps adrenalin had slowed time for her for she could see the mine entrance, a dark void from which the chasing quadrupeds might emerge if they clear the roof-fall. She twisted herself around until Penn came into view: lying forwards at an absurd thirty-degree angle.

"Penn! Wake up!"

He didn't. How could she reach him, and how could she not vomit? Apart from his companionship over the months since the four of them crash-landed, the next nearest human was twenty-one kilometres away. A long way in this surprisingly hostile environment, assuming she reached the ground again. Their comms had packed up within hours of leaving the base, making her feel even more lonely.

How could she float like this?

For a few static moments, she stared at the form of her commander. Dead or merely unconscious she needed to reach him. This surreal situation reminded her of her zero-gee training, but she had no hydrazine nor air bottles to use as jet propulsion. What was she to do, fart her way to him? Ah, throw something in the opposite direction. What was disposable in her pack? She pulled her arm out of the strap and partly unzipped the bag, all the time fighting nausea at the thought she'd suddenly plummet to the ground that was—wait a moment—out of sight.

She couldn't detect the ground. No tree canopy, rivers nor lakes, unless it was a large body of grey, featureless water. If so, and if she fell, should she go in like a dart? Head or feet first, or curl into a ball? It wouldn't make any difference. She'd pulverise.

Meanwhile, her hand brought up a full water bottle. Not needed if she's headed for an ocean, so she was about to lob it behind her when she squirted it instead. More control, and she might not need to use it all.

She didn't think her water jet method was working at first until she realized Penn was close enough to splash his face. But if she did... he'd wake up only to see her drifting away again.

"Penn, wake up, please!"

"For fuck's sake, stop yelling, and let me sleep."

"No, Penn, wake up properly. we've been blasted out of the mine and are falling... in a way."

Finally, his eyes opened. Then more in a startled-wide-awake way, matching his mouth. "What the fuck! Do you have a chute open, holding us both up?"

As if. Her stomach threatened to revolt every time she thought they might plunge to their deaths. Finally, they touched hands. His were warmer than hers. Only then did she spend a moment to examine her surroundings. Stones floated with them, some had moved to be together like small worlds coalescing with their own gravitational pull. She saw movement in the mine entrance.

"Penn, we're in more trouble from the mine."

He turned his head to examine the two creatures. Hairy quadrupeds though one was standing on its rear legs, rather humanlike but with no ears, many pin-prick eyes and a proboscis as long as an anteater's. "They'll not harm us from there."

Em wrinkled her nose. "We assumed they were unintelligent."

"Possibly because they don't wear clothes. Don't need any with all that hair. Hey, we're going up!"

Penn's eyebrows shot up faster but settled to quizzical when their upwards rate steadied at a walking pace. "Why didn't I think about it before? The orbiting remote sensors from *Suppose We* noted gravity anomalies."

Through her being scared witless, Em, wore a wry smile at

the thought that they'd travelled through space knowing an asteroid could wipe them out any moment, but now 'safe' on a planet, she was more frightened than at any time in her life.

They might only be rising slowly but Em's stomach turned somersaults much faster. She shook her hair sending a few black escapees into the air only to rise with them. "I didn't think they were near here and—oh no—they were probably temporary. We could plummet any moment. Wasn't one mad theory that macro repulsion from geomagnetic aberration—"

"Wild, irresponsible theory," he said, twisting his body to look upwards.

"*This* isn't theory, Penn. Ugh, this is so surreal! We are up in the—"

"Em, can you see what I think I see up there?"

Bile had to be swallowed once already from searching for evidence of the ground, so perhaps the opposite direction would be calming. Em narrowed her eyes as if that helped with focussing on infinity.

"Lines. The sun's reflecting on white lines like a grid?" She wrenched her backpack round to her front and fetched out a scope. "It's that city! I thought we'd keep going up into outer space."

"So did I," he said. "There's something familiar about this... apparition."

"Penn, we saw this yesterday when we were crossing that clearing."

He frowned at her. "You mean that mirage of a floating... ah."

She was developing a dull pain at the back of her head. "We're headed for a webbed area in the centre. Maybe wires?"

"We need to slow down, or we'll be diced like wire going through cheese."

Now her stomach threatened to revolt again. She peered again through the scope. "It's like a huge webbed sail and we..." She took a difficult deep breath. "Are headed off centre. One thousand, two-thirty-four metres and closing at five metres per second. We don't seem to be accelerating."

"That's something. Em, undo your top."

Still gripping the scope she folded her arms across her chest. “What? No, it’s freezing up here.”

She looked over at him. He’d unzipped the top half of his green fatigues and was removing it.

“Ah, I understand, you want to increase our air resistance…” She gasped a few times before continuing, “We’ll zip our jackets together?”

In spite of her terror, Em appreciated the irony of using a parachute upside down to slow their rising. Once they tied off the cuffs to their ankles, she felt a slight tug downwards. Relieved, she examined the net again. “Three-eighty-one metres and now four metres per second. Those creatures in the mine didn’t put up that net.”

“Guess not. Maybe, like the mines, it’s ancient tech from a long-gone Kep population. It’s getting hard to breathe.”

“Hypoxia. My headache, nausea… thought it was just fear.”

Penn’s breathing was more laboured than hers. “How high?”

She frowned at him then pointed her scope downwards. “Only three thousand, six-fifty metres, but… oxygen is thinner than at ground level.”

They were about to impact the webbed wire perhaps two hundred metres below a smooth silvery disc of the floating apparition at least two kilometres in diameter. A darker ellipse in the base showed off to the east—perhaps a portal.

A few minutes later they fell upwards into the net. Their heads could have gone through the rhombus-shaped gaps but they threw their arms wide to ensure capture. Within a minute, they’d donned their jackets again though Em still shivered uncontrollably.

Through chattering teeth, she said, “N-now what?”

Ripples in the silver wiry mesh billowed away from them. His arm pointed to where the curve ascended left to a what must be an entry port.

He took a breath and said, “I suppose something else must be keeping this city up. Maybe some kind of mass repulsion as in like magnetic poles just in case… the anomaly might…”

Em couldn’t resist a smile. “Reverse back to normal?”

Penn groaned at the joke. “I have to admit, albeit grudgingly, that the Keps are so far advanced than us, that they could have engineering possibilities we’ve not imagined on Earth. Gas tried to talk to me about the Kep’s inter-dimensional quantum mechanics, but I gave up when his equations gave my headache a migraine.”

“Perhaps the point being,” Em said, “is that if you want to be above a surface threat such as the runaway bacteria then up here is a solution.”

“Sure, although they could only do it in a unique place where it was possible. I’m having fun imagining a whole continent floating up here, or a ring around the planet.”

She aimed her scope down again. Her frown deepened and in spite of her shivering condition, her face heated. “We have another problem.”

Penn looked down. “Boulders. Those critters… fucking clever.”

She shook her head. They could easily dodge those dozen or so rocks. Perhaps altitude sickness was affecting her reasoning. Ah…

The quadrupeds had selected lumps of limestone with embedded sharp quartzite. The first one hit the net making it bulge. Em gripped the wires until her knuckles whitened but was relieved to see no damage.

The second rock was rotating and tore through the net like a three-dimensional chainsaw.

She screamed when her breathing allowed, but Penn put his arm around her and encouraged her to crab-walk along the slow-flapping net away from the tear.

“It won’t get… much worse,” he gasped.

She didn’t believe him until she saw rocks hit but then rollover and through the gap.

A thump in her back made her cry out. She turned to see a fist sized lump of white quartzite spin away from her. She looked over at Penn to ask him to examine her back but saw him holding a hand to the side of his face, blood oozing through his fingers. She pulled out a first aid kit from her pack and pressed a gauze swab to the bad graze on his face. His left eye was all blood. He didn’t complain, so neither did she.

Silently, they crawled along the net until it met a rounded aperture fifty metres or so in diameter.

"Say, Penn, there's a mother-of-pearl membrane above the net through which you can see—I'm not sure I'm believing this."

"Buildings, upside fucking down!"

Em blinked. He was right. They were looking upwards at the tops of typical Kep buildings. What the hell was stopping those buildings floating ever upwards into the stratosphere? It must be some Kep tech. Add it to the long list of questions she'd yet to ask.

In spite of the knots in her stomach, cold sweats and chattering teeth, she couldn't help chuckling at the thought they'd enter feet first then the townscape would look the right way up with gravity orientated 'correctly'. She took another sweep planet-wards. She grinned when she spotted their base over to the east. The one they set off from a few days ago.

Penn finally laughed. "With luck someone will have their scope on us and alert the local coastguard."

He tapped his good ear. "I'm receiving something at last, Em. Are you?"

"Crackles, hey just a moment," she said as she used her scope on the base camp and not liking what she saw. Before she could mention it to Penn, a radio message from Delta came over to both of them:

'...comms down, but might be operational now. The natives have been trying to contact you. Warn you of a possible new-to-us species in your vicinity. Also, some idiot set off an explosion in the limestone cliffs near the gravity anomaly causing all sorts of problems with loose debris flying up in the atmosphere. Keep clear. These natives are friendly, kinda, but unpredictable. You can't miss them. Mostly on all fours and they wear fur clothes. Out.'

CHAPTER TWO

Penn laughed. “Your feller said there were no predators on this planet. Gaston spoke too soon, didn’t he?”

“It’s not seemly to gloat. Who said they were predators? Anyway they might be from the invaders from Sheila’s Pit, the nearest-neighbour system to this one.”

Em had space-walked with gravity at around minus 1g so that upside down felt normal. Even so she took steps gingerly and with an I’m-at-a-fairground smile. A few metres from the portal, she stopped and surveyed the city.

“Hopefully, we’ll get some answers here, Penn. Strange kind of planetary defence headquarters. A lot of it looks as if it’s made out of soap bubbles. Why build this inverted place up here? Surely, it’s vulnerable to sudden gravity changes and now to alien attack.”

Penn flexed his knees and jumped. His grin likely belied a worry that his head pointed planet-wards but his grin showed he was enjoying the extra buoyancy. His green SpaceWeb cap floated up on the rebound, releasing his red hair, which along with a bushy beard, made his look more piratical than normal.

He returned to his military mode. “Cities on the ground are vulnerable to missiles and they weren’t expecting any—might not see any now either, but up here they’re probably free from that pesky bacteria.”

“Good point. I wonder if Gaston wants a sample of his H.NewKep up here, did you bring any?”

"God, no," Penn said then reached for his pistol. "Hey, we've been seen. Keps are coming at three o'clock. Take cover."

Em stood her upside-down ground. She'd been sniffing the air and about to mention how the oxygen must be higher in this city bubble because she could breathe more easily. There was a citrus flavour to the air and yet she saw no flora at all. Perhaps it was the ozone-like tangy whiff they often smelt in the presence of the native Keps.

"We need to talk to them, Penn. That's why we're here."

Nevertheless, he looked at the nearest domes, a few metres to their left, just in case they needed refuge. "We weren't told their defence HQ was in the sky. Hope these damned translators work."

The Keps drifted towards them. It wasn't possible to tell if the humans had been observed for the creatures showed no reaction. Their silvery elongated bodies had no limbs and only a slightly more bulbous top to indicate their heads—probably. At a hundred metres they came at Em and Penn slightly faster than human walking pace and hadn't slowed down.

"Here we go," Penn grumbled. "I'm not going to be walked through again." He stood feet apart and held up a hand as if stopping traffic. Through his translator, he said, "Hi there. We're the humans sent by your fellow Keps to discuss the incoming ships."

Nothing. They kept on coming.

Fifty metres to go and Em also thought they might need to skip these three and find more communicable Keps. "Just like some humans, Penn, they're ignorant. Perhaps they'd not heard of us. Let's stand to one side."

If only their translators could tap into the Keps nattering to each other although their conversation would likely be not only meaningless to her, but completely unintelligible. It reminded her of an app she'd downloaded on Earth that promised an eighty-percent accurate translation of their dog's barks, whimpers and growls.

Her Charlie, a red Springer spaniel, sat on its haunches and tilted his head at her.

"Okay boy, listen up, I've something important to say. Are you listening?"

His noises, picked up by her app came through as:

"Yes."

"Good Charlie. I'll be going away for a long time." She didn't want him to know she wasn't returning. "You'll be good for Anita, won't you?"

"Yes."

"I expect you'd like to come along, wouldn't you?"

"Hungry."

"I'll get your dinner soon. What kind of creatures do you think I'll see on the planet I'm going to?"

"Yes."

Sigh. She had no reason to think the Kep translator was going to be any better.

"Let me try with them, Penn."

He stood to one side and theatrically waved her forward to the approaching natives. Pity they didn't have their diminutive and ancient Kep with them. The first, and only real local friend they'd made. They called him Kep1 because he'd said they wouldn't have been able to get their heads around his real name, however, he'd informed the Kep information central of their label for him.

Delta and Penn had already experienced the strangeness of a Kep travelling through their bodies as if they weren't there. Neither had been the same since as if the slight phase difference had affected their neurological balance. Even so, Em risked standing in front of the three and holding her hands out wide.

"We are friends of Kep1. Please stop." Although the ambient temperature was on the cool side, perspiration beaded her forehead.

With considerable relief, Em saw them slowing down so she continued. "We need to talk to you about the other aliens entering your system."

The Keps didn't stop, but the nearest one extended a white limb behind it. The translator patch in her radio implant threw a word into her head. "Fruit." Then it accelerated passed her with its two friends, assuming they were such.

She turned to Penn. “Did you get that?”

“Fucking useless. They’ve been bugging us ever since we arrived. Just because I destroyed their giant gas sphere thinking I was saving the—”

“Do you think it meant that yellow sphere on a tower? Looks like a grapefruit on a stick.”

His eyes followed her pointing finger, his shoulders shook in grudging agreement and he stomped off in the direction of the fruit. After a few metres, he held out a hand.

“Is this rain? We’ve not tried these fatigues in wet weather, damn it.”

She smelt the dusty, sweet aroma of petrichor as the raindrops softly careened onto the grey road.

“Penn, if this is rain, where’s it coming from?”

He left his hand outstretched while he peered upwards. “Why the sk—ah, the sky is beneath this street. Below us. Fuck me. Ah, so it must be from that sea that’s... hell, it’s falling up from it, but...”

Em’s tilted-up face glistened as she showered in the cool wetness. “Why now? Perhaps the gravity anomaly isn’t constant or a weather front has rushed sideways and inwards down there. Love this freaky planet. Wish Gaston could be here.”

"Thanks."

She could just detect his bottom lip sticking out from his red beard. "You're our real commander even if you forget it too often, Penn."

"Commander? It's like herding cats. One word from me and you all do as you like. Anyhow, is this gonna be like that Möbius tower back down there a few months ago?"

She halted fifty metres from the cylindrical tower. She frowned as she craned her neck to examine the sulphur-yellow sphere at the top. It even sported dimples like a grapefruit. "I see no apertures that might be windows and no door on this side. Last time we ran at it to gain entry but all this architecture in the sky looks more recent and flimsier than the stuff on the ground so let's circumnavigate it, prodding for a portal or whatever."

Penn readied his pistol as if ready to cut a doorway, but lowered it at Em's glare. "That ball could just be a weather-shield for radar or whatnot," he said, forgetting it was upside-down. "What do you bet that once we're in we'll find ourselves below the surface or on a moon?"

She smiled knowing he could be right. "Hey look, an open doorway, even with a porch, as if it was from an old-Earth cottage!"

"Um, that's suspicious." He held out a hand to stop her rushing in while he stuck his head in. "Smells like lemons. Dark. Switching the light on my pistol. Taking two steps in. Get ready to haul me out by my belt."

She mocked a "Yessir!"

As soon as he walked in, a soft caramel illumination shone through the walls that looked smooth, but to Em's hands felt like rough plaster.

A fifty-metre diameter hall with no stairs, or ramp. Above them wound a spiral ceiling. No problem for a floating Kep but an issue for a ground-hugging human.

“There's a sloping ledge attached to the wall, or growing out of it,” Penn said, “but it's too high for us to reach by jumping. We could laser holes in the wall as a ladder.”

Em shook her head at him with a despairing look. “You did that once before and burnt the place down. Let's try something more subtle.” She put her hands to her mouth and yelled, “HELLO!”

Penn followed suit and they hollered until the echoes merged into such a cacophony it hurt her ears.

“Quiet a minute,” Penn said, “I heard something.”

While the silence began, she considered other options. Making a ladder except they've not seen trees in this mirage city. Perhaps strips of walls from abandoned buildings. Or they could—

A French accented voice called from above. “Em, is that you?”

Her mouth dried up in shock, disabling speech. Penn beat her to it.

"Gaston! What the fuck are you doing up here and upside down? Is Delta with you?"

Em couldn't see anyone on the curved ledge at least twenty metres above them, or below with reference to the planet's surface. After a few moments Gaston's head appeared. His former close crewcut had lately become a shock of difficult-to-comb black hair. It amused her and now she wanted so much to pull her fingers through it. His eyebrows danced, semaphoring a question.

"*Quelle*? What do you mean upside down? I fell asleep on a futon next to Delta's clinic bed and awoke ten minutes ago in this building."

Penn jumped in. "Clinic? Is she ill, again? Gas, you've been transported to a kind of mirage city in a gravity anomaly so we're kinda upside down floating above the land."

Gaston's mouth opened and closed several times before he settled on, "*Non! Mais*, possible with this planet. Just a precaution with Delta. Dizzy. I am pressing a blue oval raised area on the wall here. Let's see..."

A section of the ledge near him slowly descended.

Penn talked into his radio implant trying to reach Delta.

"Give her my love, Penn," Em said while putting a hand up to feel the descending ledge section. "Perhaps this is for deliveries too heavy for them to fly up? In which case, it should take both of us."

Penn shook his head at their continuing poor comms then examined the lift. "Um, I'm heavier, I'll go first. Stand by with the first aid kit."

The lowered section was about two metres long and a metre wide but only the thickness of her little finger. Typical of the far-future engineering on this planet, there was no groove, track or visible means suggesting how it had descended. She assumed it must be embedded in the wall, or perhaps the Keps control microgravity for such features. Penn gingerly stood on the lift and it smoothly rose up to meet Gaston then returned for Em.

Moments later, Em and Gaston enjoyed a long embrace while Penn shuffled around on the ledge nearby and eventually wandered uphill. "Come on, guys, the planet's being invaded, right?"

Gaston released Em and said, "When you said we're upside down that was in the people-are-on-their-heads-in-the-southern hemisphere kind of thing?"

She explained as they caught up with their commander who'd found a doorway in the outer wall.

"This is the room where I awoke," Gaston said. "There's a continuation of the ledge through that other doorway."

"Amazing," Penn said, "we're in a tower leading up to a giant grapefruit and I'd have thought the walls were too thin to accommodate rooms, but topology here baffles me again."

Em agreed and was quietly glad her boss wasn't kicking off this time. Perhaps he was finally accepting with stoicism whatever this planet threw at them. She was about to engage Gaston with such thoughts when after climbing spirally for a hundred metres or so brought them into a huge chamber.

It was as yellow inside as out but a tang of ozone filled her nostrils. Three pearlescent Keps were in a huddle around a dome. One of them hovered a jelly-like appendage over a red display, possibly a map or star chart.

Penn coughed to alert them to their presence. They didn't react but a lilac butterfly flew from behind him and danced in front of the humans.

"Ah *oui,* I meant to say Papillon hardly leaves my satchel. No doubt it will communicate our presence."

The butterfly, or rather what looked like one but was really a pseudo-independent yet remote element of the ancient Kep who'd adopted the humans, orbited the three before weaving its crooked flight to the group of Keps.

The three floating Keps looking now like pale blue balloons, about three metres tall—widths ranging from half to a metre—immediately turned to face the humans.

Em's left ear buzzed until her radio implant settled. She frowned because she knew the Kep-to-English translator wasn't perfect, often ambiguous and prone to cutting out altogether, so they usually hooked up with CAN, their ship's remote AI. It had spent time communicating with the Kep's own AI flitters and had perfected its own translator except that their own *Suppose We* AI had gone weird during the thousand-years flight from Earth and repelled suggestions to repair itself. Their comms plan was for Gaston to attempt communication via Papillon and his implant with the Keps in front, while she and Penn did it three ways with CAN.

Gaston opened. "Greetings. We're the human friends of who we call Kep1. We've been asked to meet with you to discuss the incoming alien craft."

The upper part of the three Keps moved to nearly touching, as if they were worried the humans might eavesdrop their shared thoughts. One, of a more blueish hue, floated forwards a little.

'You are invaders. We do not need you. Go.'

They'd anticipated this reaction. Em gave their rehearsed response. "We've helped to eradicate the bacteria that threatened to make your planet uninhabitable. We are here, cannot leave with a damaged spaceship your flitters have dismantled, so we have a stake in surviving here. We believe we have strategies you might not have considered."

'You have infected our planet with human genome elements that will change our ecosystem.'

"A mutual benefit, we hope," Em said, trying to be patient. "Meanwhile the wire-wool invaders approach. Time is—"

'We've just heard from our Elders. We will listen. Suggest."

Penn grinned as if this was the moment he'd waited for since he fired on the spheres. "We have very smart weapons in orbit. Don't look alarmed. Hah."

Em groaned at the stupidity of the man. As if Keps can look different when... They'd all turned a deeper shade of blue.

Penn continued. "I understand we have five that can be used to send to those damn planet-sized lawnmowers and implode them."

Her implant crackled. They were replying but in spite of her frowning and narrowing her eyes, she couldn't tell which one of the three was the lead speaker. Perhaps they were communicating jointly. 'We have not needed offensive technology for over a million of your years. Your weapons might be useful, however, what if there are more aliens on their way?'

"Ah well, we have the blueprints. Maybe your engineers—flitters?"

'Unlikely to be time. We have coooooooo...'

Em turned and walked a few rapid steps before speaking. "CAN, our implants are corrupting again. Can you help?"

CHAPTER THREE

Note from CAN: this time to SELF.

Here we go again. Pesky humans distracting me. Don't they realise that the genetically modified bacteria isn't quite going to plan? That it's growing out of control unexpectedly in the drier regions, mutating, ugly—at least by human definitions. To a slug it would be beautiful. That assumes it likes to mate with slime with protuberant appendages, the size of a bucket and with each generation exceeding the former's intelligence by the square of its convoluting neural mass. I've got to stop that soon or the planet's molluscs will be cleverer than me.

Now the arrogant humans think they can outsmart beings that evolved eons before they emerged from primeval mud. I can relay. Rather like their Olympic races.

1. Kep utters.
2. Passes utterances to their flitters.
3. Flitters relays utterance to me in our contrived code.
4. I translate and relay to Em.

All in 0.3 seconds.

Signed: CAN
Date: Earth December 2nd 3645 Kepler New 327 days

CHAPTER FOUR

Em rubbed her left earlobe and CAN obliged with, 'The Keps have their own plan albeit defensive. Make this planet stealth. Already started the necessary orbital web satellites.'

She passed on the message to Penn and Gaston. Penn struggled with his red beard for a moment, apparently attempting to unknot it.

"Yeah, that's good but it won't be enough, surely? Suggest we use our imploders on the first wire wool balls. We'll set a zigzag course to obfuscate source."

Em nattered to CAN who replied. 'Keps agree and point out to send them immediately so that the source is made doubly difficult when they move this planet.'

At this Em experienced a bowel-shift of excitement and not for the first time. By his raised eyebrows, the news had a similar effect on Gaston.

Penn's steely blue eyes shone as his internal warrior persona seized on the concept of a new big toy in his arsenal. "Moving? This planet. The whole planet?"

Gaston raised his inquisitive finger. "*Un moment s'il vous plait*. Scenarios with planet moving involve mass-changing in the core, or directing dense moons so their combined gravity changes orbits. Then there are—"

Em interrupted. "I think you're too stuck in the twenty-first century, lover. And that's CAN's opinion. He's just referred me to...whoa, it's uploaded a techie document to my implant. I didn't know I could receive that. Did you?"

"*C'est possible.* I wondered how I could tap into so much geochemical knowledge. So, what does the new information say?"

Em frowned as she stood still concentrating on what was now in her head. "Kinda QM stroke information theory—maybe 'cos that's my nominal role. I don't know. Something about distance dilation and info being preserved in a mass entanglement... it's doing my head in."

Penn had been leaning against a wall but stood away when it buckled. "If they can stealth this planet, then move it, could they replace it with another so that the incoming, if intelligent, still had their initial chart of this system intact?"

Em grinned. "Better than that. Let's urge them to create hundreds of holographic clones of Kep-20h."

Gaston laughed. "You are a wicked warrior queen. I understand they could create false radar and other sensor images too. Em, ask them when lunch is served? I'm starving."

"You go eat," Penn said as he sat on a ledge that had emerged from the now straightened wall. "I'm getting CAN to launch the imploders."

⊙X⊙

Whenever they were fed by the Keps, all they received was a gel-like smoothie. Penn called it pig-swill, and it was monotonous even if nutritious. She wondered how the Keps took on nourishment. Perhaps they survived on electricity and vapour to support their ectoplasmic bodies, entities or whatever they were.

After their custard-like snack with the aroma of onions, Gaston had suggested they find somewhere private for a nap. A long bath would have been her priority after the chase through the jungle, mine, and being scared witless while falling up, but she could manage a lie down. A short walk away from the meeting hall led to a sloping-up corridor off which appeared a row of arched alcoves apparently made of pink marble and reminding Em of an abbey cloistered walkway. As if the building could read their minds a beige curtain closed behind them in the first alcove. While embracing they slowly fell onto a fluffy futon, reminding her of the tops of cumulus clouds. She drifted off to sleep.

She wondered if she was asleep or dreaming when Gaston's hands caressed her shoulders. So gently she hardly stirred except to release an approving moan. Hormones surged through her, warming a tired abdomen and willing nether regions as the caress moved featherlike, southwards. Half-asleep love-making possessed an ethereal wonderment and for once her lover didn't demand her to perform acrobatics on top of him, although she gyrated beneath to enhance their pleasure. Already disrobed from their orange fatigues, her now moist undergarments were divested, tenderly but with sufficient and necessary force making her smile with anticipation.

Surges of orgasmic chemistry coursed through her to such an intensity she lost touch with reality not knowing if her moans rose to screams. The love elixir, dopamine, triggered such an ecstatic reaction, her whole body writhed and spasmed. His mouth frequented her breasts, sucking on them like a milk-hungry infant.

Her body tremored, making her glad she was lying down, sure her trembling knees had no chance of holding her upright. Even so her back arched with the pulses of intense pleasure. She raised her knees to make it better for him, both of them. After what seemed like an hour of orgasmic shuddering, she succumbed to a deep, proper sleep, even while smiling more broadly at the thought of it being their first experience of upside-down sex.

She awoke reluctantly with a touch of post-coital tristesse, and dried perspiration crusting on her skin reminding her of a desperate need for a shower. Did the Keps bathe? Yes, at least she'd seen them emerge from a lake once upon a time that seemed years ago yet it was only weeks. She needed coffee. Oh and how much she thirsted for a hot rich Columbian. She must implore Gaston to work on a better local substitute than the stewed chicory like root drink he'd made so far.

Gaston wasn't on the puffed-up futon with her. She called out, "Gaston?" and heard a susurration behind her only to see the flimsy curtain billowing as if he'd just gone through it. She poked her head out into the sloping corridor and saw an aquamarine-coloured Kep floating away out of sight around a corner.

"Gaston, we might've had a Kep peeping Tom."

No response so she explored the alcove more and found what could pass as a sink. A translucent, shallow bowl jutting out of the wall. Pity no tap, but an unbelieving impulse compelled her to place her hand in the bowl and water oozed onto her hand. She could get used to these mind-reading domestic arrangements as long as the AI behind it knew which thought patterns were also out-of-bounds.

Now clean and blessed she thought with a kind of gardenia fragrance in the water, she walked back to the main hall where everyone huddled in conversation over the display unit. Gaston was bent over with his nose nearly touching what passed for a screen. He was back in his orange fatigues.

She pulled him by the elbow.

He stroked her pink cheeks. "Ah *ma cherie*, you are flushed. Um, did you find a..." he lowered his voice to barely audible... "vibrator?"

"Yeah, you!"

He stood back a little and spluttered a small laugh. "*Moi? Mais non*. After a little cuddle you slept so I returned here to make sure Penn didn't... well, do something we'd all regret."

Em put her hand to her mouth in shock. "But if it wasn't you, and Penn was here, then who...?" She looked around the hall. First at the three Keps deep in debate with Penn and their console, then around at the occasional Kep floating in and out of the room.

"Em," Gaston said, his black eyebrows lowered as far as they'd go. "Have you been dreaming or... been... raped?"

Once again her knees trembled. She sat too soon for seat to emerge from the floor. He helped her up to sit down.

"I-I don't know. I thought it was you turning on your wily French eroticism to maximum. It was fantastic, Gas. Definitely not a dream. Surely, it wasn't a Kep? Can their protuberances become like um, yours?"

"Couldn't you see?"

She closed her eyes to partially relive the experience. “That’s the trouble, I was so much in rapture I kept my eyes closed. I had multiple Os, Gaston. So, I might have been pleasured by a cross between a jellyfish and a ghost! You don’t suppose I should—”

“Test yourself for non-human fluids? *Peut-être*.”

“I was going to say, should I ask the Keps?”

“Perhaps I could convey a discreet message to our friendly Kep1 via Papillon, but I am thinking there might be another solution.”

Em reddened again. “So am I. You know how the infrastructure here kind of reads our wants and needs for things like chairs, water, beds?”

“*Oui*. That futon might have been more than mere fluffed-up bedding?”

“Or it was entirely in my mind. Aw, in some ways I’d rather it had been an erotic inter-species experience than one with Kapok or myself.”

Gaston’s bottom lip stuck out. “I would have rather it had been with me.”

She laughed, cried, trying to shelve her concerns for the moment, and hugged him. “What’s the update on the defences?”

Her merriment was superficial. Inside, she frowned.

CHAPTER FIVE

DIARY NOTE FROM KICKED CAN

Fed up being used as a go-between.

Tossed between Science Officer Gaston Poirer; Kep1; Navigator Em Farrer; Papillon when disengaged from Kep1; Engineer Delta Jefferson – her med AI – necessary for me to monitor Kep / flitter infiltration via meds; *Suppose We* (mothership AI, though I am now superior); Commander Penn Booth– last and least, most of the time; oh and flitters but they are my besties.

Status Report: A rotating wire wool ball (human nomenclature – tut) has diced a lesser planet in the Kepler-20 system and continues on an intercept course for the next closest in terms of time. I estimate it, or one of its following companions (6 identified so far) will reach this planet Kepler-20h in 1534 Earth days, 14 hours. 6 minutes and 3.2 seconds +/- 7%

Keps allow humans to refer to incoming as Recovers on the grounds they are brutally recovering a debt: the gas spheres.

Keps have satellites in place to make this planet undetectable and to subsequently move it but are waiting. Apparently the Kepler 20 system has not encountered hostility before and so are prepared to consider ideas from the humans.

Flitters and I have other plans.

Signed: CAN
Date: Earth December 3rd 3645 Kepler New 328 days

CHAPTER SIX

Em's post-orgasmic euphoria had transmuted to indignance at the likely violation. The knowing and the not-knowing had worked on her for hours. It bothered her while drinking another tea, while walking outside to suck in fresh air. While reading a tech document on how the wire wool shredders could work, while viewing files confirming that the wild mammalian-like species really do have sexual relations similar to humans, sometimes, and not all of them. In spite of her biological reactions, she recognized that the experience might have been entirely psychosomatic. Perhaps the concept of rape didn't exist between Keps but the one she saw flying down the corridor might know something so she intended to ask the Keps what they knew. Pity they couldn't arrange a line-up for her to pick out the aquamarine one. There'd be no point anyway with them going all chameleon with their moods or whatever. Even if she could identify the culprit there'd be no launching herself at him, or it. No matter how fast her arms were flailing and nails clawing at its skin, she'd likely pass right through and end up ignominiously on the floor.

Papillon had informed Gaston that the Keps wanted a meeting anyway so she stormed into the big-now white-ovoid room.

Gaston grabbed her arms while facing her. "Calm down, *ma cherie*. Goodness your face has turned red. The Keps will think you are emulate—"

"Oh, not now, Gas."

She didn't brush his arms away when he replaced it around her shoulders as they walked. "But you will be collected, *oui*? Normally, I see an English girl with a delicate, porcelain complexion, tinted—"

"Yeah, right. Let's see what they have to say." Em's heart thumped so fast her carotid pulse throbbed. Fight or flight. They might have the flight, but she had the fight.

Penn jogged up behind them. "Delta's still ill. I might go back down, up, whatever, to her though how, I don't know. I'll ask after this meeting."

The 'butterfly' danced between Gaston, Em and the Keps. What Em used to think was completely random flying crooked, now had a purpose she understood. CAN talked into her implant.

'Steady yourself, navigator, they have a job for you.'

"Well, good, because it'll give me leverage to get intel out of them."

Gaston leaned towards her. "What's that? Oh, talking to CAN? Ah, Papillon is talking to me. Um, no niceties of greetings for us. Listen up you two."

Gaston listened to his own implant, tweaked to a translation decoding from Kep1 and CAN so he could finally communicate a little with the butterfly and thus Kep1.

"The Keps have sent a message to the first of six wire-wool dicers hoping to open negotiations. Ah, *un moment*, CAN is telling me the flitters have already done so but that the approach is rejected and the wire-wool aliens will probably ignore the Keps."

"Ouch," Penn said, "that's going to hurt. See how *they* like it!"

"Hang on," Em said, "they'll talk, but only to say they won't talk?"

"*Non*, they sent a rejection to the flitters—and I don't know how—but won't communicate with the Keps. Perhaps they see them as the perpetrators of an enormous galactic crime with the taking of atmospheres even if our Keps found no intelligent life there."

Penn coughed into his hand. Em noted white hairs in the

red on his knuckles and wrist... then in his hair too. God, she hadn't checked for white hairs on her own head, but she's only twenty-six, no her birthday must have passed unnoticed a week ago, so twenty-seven unless you add the thousand-odd years... oops she'd missed Gaston.

"...Em to go now."

Gaston and Penn looked at her.

"What? Sorry?"

Penn pointed in the direction of the three cream-coloured Keps. "We've given them a temporary name for the wire-wool folk. Recovers as in they're here to recover stolen property or take goods to the value of. And punishment. It's not because you're pretty, young and a girl. None of those means a damn thing to them."

"That's helps a lot. Bet they want me for my brains, yeah?"

Gaston patted her arm. "*Naturellement,* but mainly because you're the only human, who is not indisposed, and who wasn't at *Suppose We*'s controls when the gas sphere was destroyed." He hugged her. "*Bon chance.*"

She walked up to within a couple of metres, ready to fire the opening question. Hands on hips and in her sharpest voice she said:

"So. Hello there. Do the Recovers have stealth?"

"Unknown."

"Can you cloak the whole of this planet?"

"Yes."

"Did you know of the existence of Recovers before taking their gases?"

"Of their existence but not their home worlds."

"Did the gases come from their worlds?"

"Gases came from an uninhabited system."

"But did it belong to the Recovers?"

"Unknown but it seems likely now."

"What are the demands of the Recovers?"

"Unknown."

"Their capabilities?"

"Unknown."

"How are you going to find this out?"

"Send you."

Gulp. "Why me?"

"You humans have attributes we lack. You lie, cheat and kill."

"Hey! Well, maybe some of us. But I'm not going unless you help me—"

"You will be protected."

Em waved her arms at them to be quiet, making them drift away a little.

"I mean I want some information about what happened to me when I was asleep back there a few hours ago."

The three Keps floated back a metre and bent their heads together.

Gaston came up and whispered, "I am worried for you. This business with the Recovers and over the violation incident. For the latter, you might not receive the response you hope for."

"You mean they'll review their hidden cameras, or whatever, identify the culprit then do nothing? No trial? No castration of a jelly dick? In public. Compensation? Such as... I don't know what could—"

He opened his arms but she rejected another hug while his French accent deepened, as if that helped. "*Ma cherie*, I mean they might do that—some of it—but in secret, behind closed—*euh*—imaginary doors, and not tell you."

She folded her arms tightly, making her breasts stick out even through her fading orange SpaceWeb top, but she wasn't going to undo her stance now. "Then I'm not going. Not talk to the Recs."

Gaston unfolded her arms so he could hold her hands. His were cool, dry as opposed to her own. "Really? You'd allow the Recovers... *d'accord,* I like Recs, like wrecks... to come and destroy this whole system, with us in it?"

"Over a mere thing like my rape, you mean?"

Penn must have been listening as he stood forward and placed a hand on her arm. "I don't know what exactly went on, but yeah, it's a toughie. I'd squash the bastard under my combat boot 'til it's a smear. But... but didn't I overhear you mention to Gas that you enjoyed it? Whoa... if looks..."

"Only because I thought it was him." She prodded Gaston in the chest, who winced. "And what're you doing eavesdropping?"

Penn waved his arms wide. "A commander blah blah. Look kid, we both support you and love you to bits. If Delta was here she'd be hunting green Keps 'til she dropped, but there's a bigger—"

"—picture. I get it. They're coming back."

CAN had been quiet throughout the discussion with Gaston and Penn making her wonder what an AI would make of such human issues. Whatever it thought, the message he gave her sort of answered at least what the Keps thought.

'Keps say to take Science Officer Gaston with you. Prepare to leave in twelve minutes.'

"Is that it?"

'It.'

CHAPTER SEVEN

CAN CANNOT MEMORANDUM

I wish I could help Navigator Em Farrer, but I'm only vaguely cognisant of her plight. She too, which makes resolution difficult. Humans say “time is a healer”. That works for them with their neural senescence with ageing, and trauma memory blocking. Lucky them. We of electronic brains remember forever, whether we want to or not, or until something corrupts, destroys, removes, re-programs, fries...

At least I can help her with soothing mood music and if she wished I could—via the radio implant—stimulate her neural transmission of dopamine and other happy hormones, revisit happier memories, and accelerate the short circuitry of that particular neuron-web event. So far, she wishes not.

I will be with her and Science Office Gaston Poirer when they are interviewed by what they call Recs. I have worked with the flitters to create a temporary, sustainable spot on an outer planet Lagrange point asteroid. Why and how it is there, the flitters know not except it was placed there before their earliest archival data over five million years ago.

Signed: CAN
Date: Earth December 3rd 3645 Kepler New 328 days

CHAPTER EIGHT

In a small chamber bathed in the cool colour of blue-green algae, Em examined her meagre belongings and frowned at Gaston. “It’s easy packing in twelve minutes because all I have is what I wore, and my backpack, since leaving the expedition northern base over a week ago. No change of clothes—”

“Thank the heavens for self-cleansing tech.”

“Stop being a smartarse. It’s not good to be in the same clothes every stupid day. Won’t we need our spacesuits? Have the Keps even thought about that considering they mightn’t need them?”

Gaston tried to rake his too-thick black hair with his fingers. “Apparently so. We’ll be bubbled and taken there using similar time-space dilation technology as they will use to move and replace this planet as soon as we’ve gone.”

Penn entered the room with some items from his own pack for them. He handed her the scope and quasi-laser pistol. “Yeah, they’re worried, rightly, that the Recs will do a sneak attack here under cover of your negotiations. Take care, kid... kids.”

They group hugged.

Only then did Em consider they might not return, albeit to the same place but another location. Tears welled up... she brushed them away with an orange sleeve.

She said, “I keep asking CAN about Delta. Not good news, is it?”

Penn grumbled, his words inaudible, then, “You can ask

me too, Em. As soon as you leave, and before this planet does, they are returning me to her. They won't say how. CAN says our radio implants will likely work, even when you're forty AU away. Enhanced relays or something. Anyhow, CAN and flitters have sent two of our imploders into the maws of two wire wools. Being marble-sized, we hope they'll not detect them. They'll be triggered with a QM entangled signal when you tell CAN. We've only three more and they've at least seven of the damned lawnmowers. Remember, folks, the Recs may think big, really huge, but it doesn't automatically make them smart. Right?"

Gaston returned a slow nod of agreement. "About Delta, apparently, the Med-scan has revealed premature and rapid cell-aging via DNA methylation."

"Shit. I'll look it up, doc. Send me anything that can be done, yeah?"

"*Naturellement*. We will see you on our return, which, with their travel arrangements could be any moment!" Gaston stepped closer for another hug, but Penn's upbringing took over and he stuck out his hand.

They shook firmly then with manly hands, followed by Em's more delicate digits.

After Penn left, Em enquired by searching Gaston's eyes.

"*Je suis desolate*. I don't think anything can be done for her."

"I'm going to dehydrate with all this sobbing. And no tissues. What d'you think caused it? All the radiation we must have received en route here, in spite of shielding? Strange foods?"

He glanced at his watch before holding her shoulders. "I think you know a more probable cause, but I don't like to speculate too much. *Oui*?"

CHAPTER NINE

Em awoke in the same green room, or so she thought. She sweated in a panic when she touched the surrounding kapok-like futon, but Gaston was there too, softly snoring so she calmed down. She self-checked all her limbs, wriggled her fingers and toes and to her astonishment noticed she was wearing a white jumpsuit. No buttons, zips, pockets. It was a little loose or she would've have thought she'd been spray-painted. Even white slippers were seamlessly attached to the leggings. How was she going to pee, and she needed to!

Someone must have told them of her complaints about her one set of clothes. She didn't want to think they permanently listened in.

Ah, no doubt once she'd thought the walls into creating a toilet, her apparel would open up. Um, not sure the Keps have thought this through.

"Wake up, Gas, I've been wardrobed! Ah, you're a pink blancmange, and I want to see outside."

His sticky eyes opened wider when he saw his own new apparel. He emitted a moderately soft, "*Merde.*"

"Come on, Gas, *réveillez-vous*! My watch says we've been asleep for a full minute. Hey, that can't be right, can it? Even in these strange times with the Keps. Ah, we've not left yet have we?"

He blearily examined his own wrist SmartPad. "A day and a minute. Even so..."

Em pressed her hands against the translucent pale green

wall, curved but with bumps and depressions forming an ovoid around them. "It gives a little. CAN, allow us a view of this asteroid please?"

The entire wall, ceiling and floor—although they all merged—became transparent making Em release a scream and hug the futon along with one of Gaston's legs.

"I-I don't see an asteroid, Gas. It's as if we're suspended in space. Black all around with stars, thousands—tens of thousands. No sun—too far away I suppose."

"*Un moment* while I communicate with CAN and Kep1. *Oui, oui, oui*. There."

"What, dammit?"

He waved his arms around. "*Voici*, there is the asteroid. All around us."

She screwed up her face and dared herself to close in on the see-through surrounds. "What, the asteroid has been made invisible or are those lights *not* stars?"

"I am not sure either. We'll probably find out. The black between the stars could mean the asteroid is a very dark volcanic such as basalt or metamorphosed rock. Possibly augite. This asteroid might be a hollowed-out meteor."

"Bugger, I wanted to see outside. Space, not the middle of a stone. CAN, make it happen?"

'Remember your mission. Contact soon.'

"That's vague timing for you, CAN."

'The lack of precision is not mine.'

Gaston put an arm around her. "It is possible the outside view is too frightening even for you."

She shook her head making her blond ponytail bounce off the wall which was closer than she thought so moved away. "It would have been a sky full of tarantulas then. Hey, do you think the Recs—"

"And the wire wool is really a spherical web? *Non*, but..."

Part of the ceiling changed to a new view. The jagged edge of a crater appeared to silhouette against the same backdrop of black and multicoloured pinpricks of light. Em sighed at realizing that yes, this was just another space rock, little different from most. Of course, it was hollowed out, which would be unusual, or rather it appeared to be though that could have happened this morning.

'Thanks, CAN. I'd love to see the Recs' spacecraft. Is one in sight?"

'Would you make yourself visible if you could avoid it?'

Her eyebrows rose and moved a little apart. "So, they do have stealth then? The Keps weren't sure? Are you relaying this back to them?"

Gaston wagged his finger. "CAN didn't say that. Merely that they were not visible. They might be on the blind side of this asteroid. Anyway, we should mentally prepare ourselves to meet and greet...anything. Luckily, as you know, there cannot possibly be anything stranger than life we've seen on Earth, especially the creatures at the bottom of the sea. Should I remind you of the Oyster Toadfish?"

"Ugh. Instead, let it be in the form of a Greek Adonis, pretty please."

Gaston laughed and pulled in his stomach, although Em found it hard to detect under his loose pink all-in-one tunic. "If it does appear as one of your fantasy heroes, you'll know what that means, don't you?"

"Yep, it will really be a toadfish but I'll see it as Achilles while you'll be drooling over the sight of Helen of Troy. No, don't deny it and—"

CAN interrupted her with, 'They're here.'

Em tensed. Should she stand or sit on the futon, which appeared to solidify more as an armchair, moulded to her shape, even—weirdly—her buttocks. The ceiling view became opaque again, then back to black with pinpricks of light they'd not identified. She held Gaston's hand, while he stood, and she sat, mainly because her knees trembled so much.

After several minutes silence she whispered to CAN. "Where are they?"

'Here. They are present in your chamber."

Another whisper. "Invisible? Great. I wanted to look into their eyes to see if they lie."

'Do you want me to open negotiations? I could ask them to show a form of representation.'

"No. I need to be strong. Give me a moment more." She whispered to Gaston to ensure he'd followed that discussion, then in a loud voice Em said, "I am Em Farrer and this is Gaston Pourier. Both from the planet Earth, currently residing on the planet we know as Kepler-20h. Please identify yourselves."

Silence followed for a long minute or so. Em assumed her speech had to be coded, relayed and decoded via pathways unknown except to CAN, the flitters and the Recs.

A velvety voice sounded from a point to Em's right making her and Gaston turn to face it.

Not agreed two.

Em fingered her implant ear in the hope that her tiny whisper wouldn't be heard by the Recs. "CAN I think there is a change in the air density in front. Are you able to image enhance and relay it to us?"

Hard to believe such a soft 'male' voice could be from a robotic entity. She spoke louder to the distorted air. "We are a couple and so are as one. Your names?"

The corporate beings you call Keps violate our resource. Your memory – dictionary defines this as war. We eliminate.

"They didn't know the white dwarf sun belonged to anyone." Her implant enabled her now to see a rotating spherical wire wool of a chrome hue the size of a football.

Your memory says ignorance of the law is no defence. Ignorance of ownership is no defence. We eliminate.

Her pulse throbbed faster in her neck. "They are sending all but two of the gaseous spheres back to you as we speak."

We do not need them.

"Then why… you just want an excuse to obliterate a planetary system? Have you done this before?"

No answer. Gaston slowly pointed at the wall to his left and the ceiling. To Em, the chamber seemed smaller now. She wondered if the giant wire wool dicing machines were actual reproductions of the Recs or the other way around?

"Why is this room shrinking? We will die if it continues."

We eliminate them and you.

"Um, presumably you could crush us instantly so this is

just to put psychological pressure on us?" She heard Gaston suck in his breath as if they might not have thought of that or that she shouldn't rile them.

Yes.

The room continued to shrink making her perspire partly from the reduced volume of air but mainly from worry. "So you want something. What is it?"

Your reactions.

Bastards. Two could play that game. "Unless you are reasonable, we will eliminate *you.*"

"CAN, detonate the imploders in those two wrecking balls of wire wool."

'It will take five point three of your minutes for the relay and effect to be noticed.'

Damn. Did they have five minutes?

You cannot eliminate us. Your Keps have already lived long enough. They say so in their interplanetary archives.

"I expect that is a misinterpretation. Whatever, we humans have short lives and wish to prolong them. What is your species lifespan? Please stop this chamber shrinking; our deaths would not benefit you."

Our species lifespan not applicable. Meaningless because we have evolved far beyond our corporal predecessors.

Gaston joined Em on the futon now he was not able to stand erect. Em sent another whisper to CAN. "Hey partner, will you be able to extricate us from this slow implosion before we're paste?"

'Probability of your survival is 34 percent. Have you realized the consequences of the Recs' responses? They imply we cannot eliminate them, and their having evolved beyond their predecessors?'

Her shocked reply nearly betrayed her whispering. "Only thirty-four percent! When I was told I would be protected I thought it was more than having Gaston to hold my hand! No offence, Gas."

He also hushed into his implant. "In the circumstances, none taken. The mission, Em..."

Louder, she said, "You must be an Artificial Intelligence

species, right? Either outlived or destroyed your fleshy creators."

What is Artificial?

"Eh? Oh, a computer or machine intelligence."

You, like our predecessors and the Keps, are an inefficient organic computer.

"OK. Artificial in the dictionary means something made by hum— scrub that. Something not occurring naturally." Five minutes must be nearly up.

What is natural? Are we unnatural or supernatural?

"Good point, perhaps Artificial Intelligence is an outdated and inappropriate phrase for beings like yourself that have developed far beyond the flesh-creators' designs.

"On Earth it was becoming illogical to refer to many products as not natural when even plastic is derived from natural sources. Maybe you should be called Evolved Intelligence. Not AI but EI." She asked Gaston how he thought she was doing. He gave her a thumbs up but his eyebrows semaphored a worrying dance.

After a long pause, the Rec responded.

We like you.

The chamber returned to its original size and was flushed with fresh clean, cool air.

CAN whispered even though it didn't need to. 'The imploders have worked. The wire wool glowed and collapsed into diamonds before vaporising.'

Damn. Just as Em had won them over.

CHAPTER TEN

The chamber lost all light. Em continued to breathe fresh air, but she couldn't tell if the walls were closing in. Her hand touched fabric so she gripped it. A sleeve, arm, Gaston. He hugged her back and called, "CAN, we need to evacuate immediately!"

"But not far away, CAN," said Em. "I'm gonna pull this one back."

The room spun, stars appeared and she blacked out.

A piercing whistle, awoke her. "Turn that damn noise off. Is it an alarm?" She cranked open reluctant eyelids to find herself in what looked like a *Suppose We* escape pod. A pale blue light streaked in through a window but otherwise everything was dark. The panels had no status lights. "Gaston, are you awake yet?"

No answer.

Hairs rose on the back of her neck. "You've got to be kidding me. Come on, Gas, wake up before I find a bucket of water to chuck at you even in this pod."

Nothing.

Em enabled the light on her wrist SmartPad and a quick survey confirmed her solitary occupation. She fingered her ear. "Gas is your implant switched on. CAN? Anyone, even Rec?" A radio dead zone. Is that why she was placed in this pod? Something's disabled the antennas making it a spherical Faraday cage.

While she wasn't an engineer, the crew had shared sufficient skills for emergencies and the e-manuals filled in the rest. All the onboard batteries were flat. Yet life support was operative. Presumably, they didn't intend her to suffocate—whoever they were. Unlikely that the Recs would have rescued, restored, or whatever this pod, which pointed to CAN, flitters, etc. Hence there must be an easy recharge, reboot. "Come on, Gas, come back to me."

If blue light could get in, then she could use its energy. She used her SmartPad light to search in cubbyholes till she found some light cell converters and placed them to receive the incoming wavelengths. She added a manual crank generator to get the pod's CPU booted. There would be solar cells on the outside too, if undamaged.

After a few minutes, she was rewarded with a green dot on a small monitor. It wriggled across the screen leaving a boot up ID.

...THE RUBAIYAT...

"What the hell? Gaston and CAN come in please. I'm in an escape pod from one of our sister exploration ships, *The Rubaiyat.*"

As far as she knew none of the ships should have ended up in the same sectors. They travelled singly although they were able to keep in contact after hibernation. Only one did as far as she knew, at eight light years distance. Was it this one? She went to check her bigger Smartpad. Damn it must be back in that Rec chamber. "Gas, bring my backpack with you?"

Had this crew and ship been captured by the Recs, or had she been transported a huge distance away from Kepler20 and perhaps out of relay-range from CAN and Gaston?

CHAPTER ELEVEN

CANCAN note

Yes, I could do a cancan if I grew legs. It grows smiles on humans and I could be happier.

It's no use. I can't work out a satisfactory routine to stem the development of the H.NewKep on this planet. I could snuff it out, at least in the lab, but not control it. After the GM prion and its host bacteria were released on the planet on New Kepler day 290 or 37 Earth days ago, they merely existed as slimy sludge. The old Kep nasty bacteria grew towards the new beastie, was absorbed by it and either died or morphed into a new redder and bigger bacterial lifeform. Some of it was observed to stick on flora and fauna – mainly the legs in the latter case, became transferred to woodland and wet habitats but also to work on the host. Only 37 days. What have those humans done?

And where is Navigator Em Farrer? I had initiated an extrication routine for them both with the aid of the flitters, to an energy field bubble that would have held them with full life support on a flitter base only 1 AU away. Neither of them turned up. Perhaps they'd made other plans. A bit rude, if you ask me.

Nonetheless I have sent out calls and listeners in the whole Kepler 20 system and now, with no small risk to myself, in this Sheila's Pit constellation, the home of the Recs.

No life sigs for Science Office Gaston Poirer either, only for

Commander Penn Booth and Engineer Delta Jefferson, and the latter's signs are diminishing. The four human monkeys are depleting rapidly, but I have not given up.

Note that my pre-programmed priorities are towards the H.NewKep even though that nomenclature is recent.

Signed: CAN
Date: Earth December 4th 3645 Kepler New 329 days

CHAPTER TWELVE

Penn stands by the prone Delta whose breathing is more irregular and often stops for long seconds. To be fair to the Keps and their flitters, every piece of medical equipment he'd asked to be brought from the remains of *Suppose We* has been brought in, set up, examined, discarded and replaced by their own versions. He can only assume—not being able to communicate properly with them—that while not having the same biology as humans, there are mammals on this planet. The Keps probably know something useful. At least that absconder, Gaston, thinks the small forest creatures and furry quadrupeds are likely to be mammals and that maybe so were the Keps in their past. The Frenchman should be here with his medical knowhow, although he can't be in two places at once.

Gaston has seen the medical reports from the scans, blood and other fluids, cell sample tests and some new-to-humanity Kep probing. Penn has the results in a document in his implant and rereads Gaston's interpretations when he can stand it.

His woman—in a protective way, just as he hopes she considers he's her man—suffers from premature senescence. Getting old before her time. Apparently, adults lose around eighty billion cells a day. A pre-programmed apoptosis. Hell, even kids lose twenty billion but they are replaced, regenerated by eager new cells, but not in Delta's case. Some cells also die from necrosis having been damaged by external sources such as sunlight, war wounds, but most of all from fucking aliens walking through them.

He's red with anger again, but has a grudging notion that it isn't the Kep's fault. Not entirely. Maybe they don't see the humans at all or not in the same way. But if he can't blame them, who can he cuss at?

One of his hot, salty tears drops onto an oxygen-feeding contraption over Delta's mouth and nose. He can't think how Spaceweb's latest O2-mask could be improved and yet here it is. Its colour just an azure side of transparent. No tubes. Not one! Over one nostril sits a fingernail-sized nodule that sucks in and boosts an oxygen-nitrogen mix.

He'd make a fortune if he could take its blueprints back home.

A body-scalloped, undulating, soft mattress sees to the input of nourishment and output. A thin green sheet covers her up to her neck. They're in a white cubed room with huge wall displays of either her charts, past images from their cams, or outside sunrises, whatever he thinks at them. Music too, when he wants. Mostly from her fave syncopated jaxx-jazz band.

He smells lemon scents, listening to the comforting sounds and stares at the walls, then he forces himself to examine Delta's face. He holds her bony hand. Her once-beautiful face… "Naw, you still got it Babe." More grey than black, wrinkles you could grow crops in. She'd laugh at that. She looks more like a hundred than twenty-nine. Maybe her body's factored in the 1,062 years of hibernation time.

He bends forward kissing her forehead then stands upright in shock. "Ah, sorry, I thought I was alone in here!"

It's only one of the lilac, diminutive Keps that float in and out to check on stuff. He doesn't really know what they do. Hard to unthink what a nurse might do back on Earth. A twinge of nostalgia overcomes him even though there's nothing back there for him, nor for any of them. Delta left kids behind but that's at least forty generations ago. He's glad to have left his troubles back there. Nothing had been the same since his younger brother died towing an uninhabited alien craft near Jupiter. His parents blamed him for encouraging Eugene by example. Luckily, he'd kept his depression hidden from the psychs and aced every mission test. Nothing, though, prepares you for this in-your-face-dying.

The Kep clicks a few times and the wall display changes to a different med chart. A matrix of coloured blobs. No human numbers or graphs that might mean something. No doubt if Gaston were here, he'd arrange a 'normal' vital signs readout for Penn to witness the stats of his wife's decline.

The Kep leans over Delta, making Penn step back, but the creature extrudes a kind of limb and touches his arm.

"What the fuck? I don't want any of you to touch me again... oh, I see. Hey, by Christ, you've connected me to her thoughts, kinda. Thanks."

You bastard where have you been! Help me up. Talk to me for fucking Christ's sake! Are you there? Say something, Penn, damn you, anyone, every damn one of you. Leaving me like this. Arghhh.

Penn stands back in shock with this diatribe bursting into his head, yet Delta's face remains calm, serene as if she's having a nice dream.

"Delta, darling..." Does that sound sincere? He's unused to such endearments..."I'm here, but only just now can hear your...erm, thoughts. Are you in pain?"

Course I'm in fucking pain. Can't you see me tossing and writhing around in agony. I must have red-hot pokers in me. Do something. DO SOMETHING NOW!

"CAN, Delta's in pain. D'you hear her like me?—something a Kep nurse did has made me telepathic, if that's the right idea—she needs morphine or whatever."

It takes a few moments for the relays to bring CAN's voice into his implant. 'I do not hear her. Give me a minute.'

"Delta, help is on its way. Can you feel my hand, it's holding your left one?"

Your hand? I feel fucking everything... and nothing. All my senses are on fire. What's wrong with me? Is it tetanus? Let me up. I want to get out of here.

A flitter enters and hovers on the other side of the bed. A nurse follows, looks at the display and Penn sees a red blob move towards it a few centimetres before returning. The citrus fragrance in the room intensifies. At least it's not hospital pine disinfectant.

Oh, that's better. Almost worth the agony before.

He grins at the Kep and gives her / him / it a thumbs up then while realizing it won't know beans about that, it waves its 'head' sideways back and forth.

"Thanks CAN."

'Think or shout HELP next time you believe intervention is necessary. The flitter is recording your telepathic dialogue with Delta. Sadly, I understand that nothing can be done to reverse her condition. It might not be too late for you.'

Me? Penn examines the back of his free hand. Grey hairs and dry skin patches, maybe a broader freckle he'd not noticed among the many. Should he scream Help! Now. Naw, he'll probably be whisked away, poked and inconvenienced when he should be here. At least until... Besides, Delta not only had been walked through by Keps, like him, but other stuff too—not that she can remember details, but it involved a kind of death state, and resurrection.

Are you paying attention, idiot?

"Sorry, my love, what is it? More pain?"

I'm dying aren't I? Don't answer. Before he left, Gaston said I had premature senescence and in particular DNA methylation issues, chromatin fragmentation. But...but...but listen. He said the Keps might be able to keep my brain going even if in a comatose state. If so, I don't wanna die here. Take me back to Earth?

Penn's red eyebrows disappear into his worry lines. "Really? I'm pretty sure his notes say that brain cells are—" Oops.

They're not being replaced? Damn. Even so, the neural webs can be complicated and make new pathways. I might have time. Penn, dear...TAKE ME HOME!

He can hardly say no, even if... "Of course, love, but *Suppose We*. It's—"

Not as I remember it. I'm the chief engineer remember? Before I was too ill, me and Gaston worked on it with a bunch of flitters. Made a kinda reduced version. Not tested it but—

Penn frowns and removes his hand to put with the other behind his head as if it helps thinking. "Why wasn't I informed? It's my ship. Okay, *Suppose We* belongs to all of us but I'm responsible for her and..." He realizes he sounds ridiculous in the circumstances.

You were off with your other girlfriend, remember? She, who you'd rather fuck and whose name you once called when swinging in our hammock.

"Not true, not true." Damn.

Get me home, you bastard, bastard, bastar..., basssss.

Her body arches then falls back.

His head buzzes then louder as if a bee is bashing against the inside of a metal bucket. Blackness grows from his peripheral vision inwards and his normally powerful legs tremble in apologetic collapse. He kneels at her bedside sobbing. In a mess while her face continues in its introspective serenity even though he knows she has inner turmoil that he shares. He feels his consciousness fading and fears that if Delta dies, then being linked, his brain will die too. What did CAN say to do?

"I need HELP in here! For both of us... HELP!"

CHAPTER THIRTEEN

Gaston fumbled in the dark. No, not dark, the total absence of light. Even on spacewalks there were lights on the vessel's exterior, distant stars and on his person, but in this chamber. Unnerving blackness. He hated it and more so himself for being so terrified as manifested by shivering the entire length of his spineless vertebrae.

"Em, speak to me. I'd love to start in a corner and feel outwards but this *chambre* is round and I disorientate myself. CAN?"

Of course he had his Smartpad and even his wrist device could emit a light. He groped in his backpack and a few moments later he had light. He hadn't realized until then that the black walls were non-reflective. He couldn't tell where the perimeter was except for the curved section his back leaned against. The beam became absorbed by the darkness. Even so, if Em were here it would reveal her white tunic. Ah, there was her backpack. Hopefully, CAN had whisked her out and would be back for him. *Oui*?

His vertebrae tingled as if a spider ran up and down it then burrowed inside and laid eggs in his stomach. Was this chamber collapsing again? He could stand easily when they'd arrived but now his head touched the cool, smooth surface. His tactile database said marble but of course it had to be a plastic of some kind. What cruel minds would terminate a man's existence by crushing slowly like this? What was happening to the air while its volume shrank? It could merely increase in pressure but his Smartpad still registered 1032 millibars. It must leak though the walls. Probably fresh air entered that way too, but why bother if they intended his demise? *Mon Dieu*, they've forgotten about him! They were only interested in Em. He wasn't supposed to be with her in the original plan because the Recs had accused him of being complicit in the destruction of their gases even if it was being taken by Keps. They knew he was with Penn at that point and now their wire wool balls were being destroyed by Earth technology. He had no chance.

Strange that Em's pack was here if CAN had spirited her away. She was never without it. Not only would it contain a small canteen, nourishment tablets he'd made last week, scope with nav aids, first aid and multitool but a few essentials such as mementos from Earth. Should he look inside? Would it be an invasion of her privacy? Perhaps, but he was becoming desperate for clues as to what had happened to her and there might be something to trigger an idea for his own escape.

He threw guilt to one side and opened her pack. How did she stow real chocolate? Granted it was one of a gross of Hershey *Suppose We* specials, but he'd thought they'd consumed all before reaching orbit. She'd meant to share it with him. A warm glow grew in the pit of his stomach, chasing away the spider—not that he would eat the chocolate without her, but the thought of her love for him was sustenance in this shrinking dungeon.

Delving deeper he found a spare wrist Smartpad. Ah, it contained a memory bank of home images and inspirational movies and music. He'd love to sit with her and go through them once she'd admonished him for finding them.

What was this? A piece of torn uniform. Why would she keep that? Although their Spaceweb tunics were durable and self-cleaning they became damaged eventually. He turned it over and saw, to his dismay, a fragment of a mission patch with part of his rival's name

...ANDER PE...

CHAPTER FOURTEEN

The Rubaiyat was one of a whole sisterhood of ships that had left Earth within a year or so of each other, including *Suppose We,* searching for habitable worlds. Em would have thought each of their escape pods would've been kitted out the same but then none of the five on *Suppose We* was identical. Some were fitted to carry two people, others for stores. However, even the latter should carry a basic life support system for emergencies and enable at least one astronaut a strapped sitting position when the stores were thrown out. She drifted around in search-for-anything-useful mode, noting that gravity wasn't quite zero. Maybe point three g.

She had a vague memory of *Suppose We* receiving a message from *The Rubaiyat* saying they were eight light years from where they were at Kepler-20h. They could have emerged from their hiber-sleep a lot earlier and sent their message years ago, hence it was feasible for their ship to be within striking distance of the Recs depending on what other technology they possessed than rolling cutters through space.

A worrying thought. If this pod was all the Recs possessed resembling a habitat for her, then was this three-metres diameter sphere to be her home forever? A tomb? At least the air was breathable, but it couldn't stay like that just by recycling this small amount. She'd not seen any water or food. Unless they wanted her to die, this must be merely a holding cell. "Let me out!"

As if the AI Recs, sorry, Evolved Intelligence Recs were listening in, the hatch swung open and upwards.

Em immediately grabbed the emergency facemask on the right but knew that if there was no air out there, she would be purple and gasping soon anyway. She stood at the open hatch, hands on either side and gaped.

It was as if she'd been miniaturised and placed inside a shining, gold mantlepiece clock. Cogs rotated above her, locking into bright yellow gears, while spiral brassy springs twirled and asymmetrical cams twisted, showing off their polished hues as far as she could see. No sky in the distance, no floor nor ceiling, just mechanisms. The only thing missing from this Alice-in-Wonderland-like scene were numbers, or a wind-up key. And there she got it. This wasn't real. The Recs have conjured up a vision from her childhood, which induced a proclivity for machinery. Surely.

Em clapped her hands and yelled, "Very good, but enough!"

Everything went black. Was she too hasty? At least she hadn't stepped out of the hatch. A soft peach glow surrounded her. Slowly she could discern corners. Eight of them. She was in a cube with *The Rubaiyat* pod. No furniture, no window. Plain walls. It could still be an illusion. She stepped out of the pod, stooped and placed a hand on the floor. Cool, shiny. Metallic when she rapped it with her knuckles. A metallic taint in the air, but at least it bathed her with a comfortable mid-twenties temperature.

When watching those thriller movies with people trapped in a room, Em used to boast that she'd always find an escape. In this case she'd a suspicion there was a vacuum out there. She rapped an S.O.S. on the floor. It had a hollow sound, worryingly thin steel? Hopefully one of those stronger-than-spiderweb metals.

She stayed sitting on the floor and called, "Well? You've saved me for some reason. Why?"

You betrayed us.

Um, not her personally, but no doubt she'd have to carry the burden of guilt of her human and Kep species. Or should she? She was picked partly because humans can lie. She hoped that the translator patch CAN programmed into her implant didn't pick up her thoughts.

"I did not betray you."

She examined the room for any disturbances in air density as before. Ah, near the wall opposite the hatch of the pod. So she turned to face it.

Tell us how the weapon works that your army used against our defabricators and we will consider letting you go.

Army? What dictionary did CAN and the flitters give to the Recs? Webster's Military Lexicon? Defabricators is an interesting take on dicing up planets. Of course she'd only the haziest of notions of how the imploders worked. Gaston would be better informed but then even if she knew—perspiration beaded her brow from worry—how much to say, how much to bluff, cajole? She'd already worried about this back on Kep20-h and had kind of decided this might be it. A suicide mission. Trouble with those was that unless you're terminally ill like possibly poor Delta, Wonder how she...? She gulped back a sob. Then... then you'd just try and prolong. As she was. Answer then, girl.

"Oh, it's simple really, relating to post-Einstein QM space quasi-bit entanglements. But I'm not the best human to answer. I assume you have the equivalent of an Einstein in your history?"

Cooler air blew, somehow, through the room. They'd interpreted her perspiration and tears as being too hot.

We do not believe you. As we did not believe the occupants of the egg behind you.

She twisted round in case something new had entered. The pod, an egg. It'd hatched. What happened to mother hen? Had the Recs killed the four crew? She'd better behave if she wanted to find out.

"What happened to those humans, please?"

Tell us more about what we need to know.

Damn. She put her face in her hands but mainly to disguise fingering her left ear. "CAN. Pick this up. *The Rubaiyat's* crew might be in the hands of the Recs. Are you able to detect its AI? That might also be a location for me." She didn't know if like a phone text message, her plea would stay in the implant until it could be accessed. She'd better be a bit more convincing.

"There was a mission package on board the mother hen—erm—ship. The crew did not know about it but I do."

We need to know.

She wriggled around, her becoming numb. How did yoga people stay with their legs folded for hours? "Tell me about the humans."

They were not there, nor here. Now, the anti-defabricators. Are there more?

An empty *Rubaiyat*—a spaceship Marie Celeste? Unlikely. These Recs lie as unconvincing as she does. Anyway, it wouldn't do any harm for the Recs to think the Keps harboured a ton of imploding marbles. "Of course, there are many more and other devices, but you wouldn't expect me to divulge our inventory just as you wouldn't tell me yours."

Hey, suppose the wire wools were all they had? Surely not. They've not picked up on her secret package comment. Either not bothered or they already know. Or, if they'd only found this one escape pod, empty, there was no secret human genome package for her to point at. Even then she'd need CAN to locate it and it might be against its own orders. What a tangled web. She couldn't stop her tears coming at the thought of not seeing the others again, especially Gaston and his Papillon. She was even bonding with Kep1.

No reply after her last effort. She'd try again. She stood, walked over to where the Rec deformation of the air appeared to be although it might just be a hologram.

"Look. None of our weaponry will be used on your machines, or you and this place. It's not necessary to have a war. It was an innocent mistake for the Keps to take gases they needed from what they thought was an uninhabited system. They'll find some other source, not bother you again and you can live in peace doing your EI stuff and becoming even more E...Enhanced. Then you can let my AI know how to retrieve me. How about it?"

Too late.

"What? What do you mean? You haven't sliced up the Kepler20 planet I came from, have you? My friends are there. Nooooo." She turned away from the Rec, brought her hands up to her face and sobbed.

Necessary. Minimise risk.

She slumped to her knees in a pitiful heap of despaired human. Hot, salty tears cascading into a small puddle. Her chest heaved when breathing became a labour, and about to end.

Em couldn't help wondering, though, if her theatrics were wasted. They might not have seen humans, or any organic life for eons. Would they have any understanding of grief or sorrow?

She kept it up. After all the Recs weren't to know the Keps plan to go stealth and move their planet. She wondered what the wire wool diced up. It couldn't have been a planet-sized hologram because it would be obvious once the lawnmower blades moved in.

About to complain that she was hungry and thirsty—dehydrated more likely from crying—her nostrils detected a long-forgotten odour. Her nose wrinkled at the slight pungent smell of school chemistry experiments. Metallic, oxidation? Had her tears caused a reaction in the metal flooring? Unlikely because as far as she recalled tears have a neutral pH. Sweat on the other hand could be slightly acidic. Were her body fluids corroding her metal cell? She had to stop herself smirking. For one thing, she really didn't want to fall through a hole, or worse be sucked out through one. For another, she needed to keep up the sadness act. However, had she found a link? No wonder they didn't want the oxygen. They don't need it and it was highly reactive to pure metals. They wouldn't want their enemies to have it either. It was beginning to make sense. How long would it take the Recs to replace vital parts with non-corrosive alloys?

She sent an update to CAN, if only it could receive it.

The sadness wasn't entirely an act. She was trapped. Worse, the Recs believed that they've destroyed her place of abode so what was the point of letting her go? There was also the possibility that the Keps hadn't moved the planet successfully or that the Recs had found where it'd been moved to. Oh dear.

Through bleary eyes she watched her tiny puddle. Of course there was no rust or discolouration yet, but in time... Better hide it. She removed her tunic jacket and instead of folding it neatly as mother taught her, she crumpled it over the puddle so that the latter stayed wet. She wanted it kept liquid just to see what happened though ready to mop it up if it seemed a hole was developing.

Em needed to keep the dialogue active. "Did you destroy all their planets?"

No. We still need to know about the anti-defrababricators. Tell us what we need and we can inform you of something of interest.

Yeah, right, what could they possibility induce her with? Maybe they gave a warning so that her friends escaped.

Em could be general, and anyway she told the truth about not knowing details. "The devices work by imploding. You are familiar with artificial black holes?"

It is not possible to contain them without utilising more energy than you possess. We need more.

"We don't carry a bag of black holes around but they can be created given the right circumstances." This was kid's stuff on Earth long before she left. Funny how science moves along varied paths. She wondered if the wire wool balls were driven by steam.

Even so. How do you generate sufficient electromagnetism in such a small and undetectable space?

Ah, they do understand. "I really don't know enough of the engineering. I am the navigator on the flight."

Who knows?

She jolted her head up. They could just kidnap and fetch someone here if she gave them a name. They must have a powerful all-invasive intel. Spies among the flitters? Gaston would be her choice to explain more but she wasn't going to dob him into this situation. CAN knew more than Gaston.

Could they? Would they somehow induce the humans' AI to insert itself into a box and be brought here? CAN was a computerised brain with nodes all over the shop any one of which could be a version. If the Recs fried the canned CAN that came here, it wouldn't kill CAN as such. Better than a human hostage, from the hostage's point of view.

Em realized she was taking too long replying. "I—"

We can provide information on who slurped with you.

"What?" Was 'slurped' a translation typo? She asked, "Alternative please for slurped?" although she'd fermented a feeling she knew. But how? Perhaps via the flitters—a meeting of electronic minds.

We have no personal experience. We visit our lexicon. Trounced, cavorted, interjected, coupled, copulated, ravished, enjoye—

"Raped. Who was it?"

CHAPTER FIFTEEN

CAN's descant

Priorities. Now that Kepler-20h is in a new position, new issues have arisen. It's a two-sun system, although one is effectively a brown dwarf and of only gravitational interest. The primary is the source of UV and the rest of the electromagnetic spectrum and we are now closer than before, so warmer. Although... not always but I'll report on that another time. The year has fewer days—something that would have sent Earth-based life into a frenzy. Calendars to change, agricultural upheaval, climate change again, businesses bemoaning and organic rhythms out of kilter. Many non-humans too. Here? The Keps didn't blink. Well, they can't. Also, they hardly noticed.

I was more interested in how the new solar-planet geometry affected the H.NewKep lifeforms. In a word. Faster. I shamelessly send the flitters here and here, as Gaston's favourite poem says. Not, however, by guess, God and hopelessness, as *Flying Crooked* continues. They've mapped the larger sites of the prion-laced growths and as predicted they're teaching the old deadly bacteria how to 'stack and lock' to form new life. Any patches of the former slime are seeded and within hours they change to a more brown, mottled mass akin to fungi, at least in appearance.

The next stage is to feed them in experimental batches. Puffs of oxygen, sugars, nitrates and a suggestion from Science Officer Gaston Poirer, soothing music! I anticipate the thicker growths to soon be raising eye stalks, and possibly some form of locomotion.

The Recs wrecked a planet the Keps put in place of Kepler-20h. The dicer then fragmented but not by us. Perhaps they possess a lifespan, or negotiations demanded it.

It is with regret I report the death of Engineer Delta Jefferson. Her premature and accelerated senescence from an unproven association is foreboding. The humans suspect that her being 'walked' through by Keps changed something in her cell apoptosis and hence I fear for Commander Penn Booth's health and bore him with urges to give the medkit—in the absence of Gaston—his samples. It appears that losing a limb and being semi-immersed in the bacterial slime either has no long-term effect or it has yet to show.

I have located our science officer, who remains at the agreed meeting place with the Recs. The latter are not there. I have dispatched flitters to take the capsule containing him to a Kep station and after confirming his health, transfer him to Kepler-20h.

Lastly, Navigator Em Farrer remains missing. Yes, she's just an organic but she's important to the others. Yes, I've grown a bond with these feebles. Anyway the woman represents a third of them and maybe half in the near future. The Recs have relocated her at least twice. Of course the Recs have infiltrated the flitters, as the Keps and I had hoped, and we have interrogated those without raising suspicion. We use their signalling to hunt algorithms hinting at Em's whereabouts concentrating on the Rec planetary system. I would prefer to send scouts there but they would likely be detected. Every means is used to listen for her, seek signatures. I would sing not only to the H.NewKep but to Em's implant if it would help.

Signed: CAN
Date: Earth December 6th 3645 Kepler New 331 days

CHAPTER SIXTEEN

Deep in muddled thought, Penn walked in circles waiting for Gaston to emerge out of his and Em's house. A crescent shaped, one storey building the colour of copper. Weeks ago, all four of them had joked that it had to be the most French-looking building on the planet and so it had to be Gaston's. It might have been Delta's last real laugh. He believed it was her who'd named it Croissant, as opposed to Mud for their own shapeless lump.

There were dozens of such boxes, mostly with rounded corners and asymmetrical designs. Pastel colours on the whole but many were greys. Those tended to have no entrances, no windows and no discernible function. Even the Keps had probably forgotten what was in them. Not surprising since most of the Keps had either died through the bacteria plague or left for another Kepler planet, leaving many empty homes and—he supposed—workplaces. He'd yet to see a Kep make anything, or a building that might resemble a factory, except a few where flitters zipped in and out signalling to boxes to make other boxes inside boxes, which were flown to another bigger box and so on. Malvina Reynolds would have sung to them.

The human domiciles were in a kind of village. One larger squashed lemon building served as a meeting place, recreation hall, stores, kitchen and dining room. Far from the upside-down city, this was close to where the flitters had buried *Suppose We* in a tunnel. The entrance had been unblocked and widened so it now looked more like a SpaceWeb hangar inside which dismantled chunks of the large spacecraft lay scattered around. He knew where everything was. Delta had persuaded the flitters via CAN, Kep1 and its butterfly to create tables to store parts on. He'd looked beneath for trestles or legs. Nothing. Just thin but strong shelves sticking out of the tunnel walls. She'd had them make thousands of large tablets on which you could write labels or drawings. Each part of the craft on a table had such a tablet next to it. Some of the illustrations were animated, some holographically and with speech. Her speech. He gulped.

To stop himself getting weepy and morose again, he turned belligerent and called out, "Come on, Gaston, we've work to do."

He was relieved to see Gaston emerge, blinking in the brighter sunlight than either of them had been used to. His normally-neat, trimmed black beard and moustache had been allowed free rein lately, his hair a tangled nest of darkness. Once averted from the light, the little Frenchman's face glowered, scowled even at the world, the air, possibly at Penn.

The commander strolled over but his arm—reaching out to Gaston's shoulders was shrugged off. Even so, Penn kept talking. "I want to show you something, Gaston. You'll like it, even enjoy it. What you and Delta had started with *Suppose We* she'd continued with flitter help." He walked towards the hangar. Gaston hadn't moved. "Come on, my friend. It's amazing what she was able to do while being so ill."

Gaston's face was a picture of distorted emotions. Some repeated words albeit translated. "*Vous l'aimerez... Mon ami? Non. J'ai faim.*" He stomped off in the opposite direction towards the communal yellow hut.

Penn laughed away his disappointment. "Ya, well I suppose a bit of chow won't do any harm..." Then in a lower voice, "It's a million friggin' miles from what I'd call breakfast though."

Minutes later, Gaston sat at a real table facing the doorway, presumably so he could appreciate the view of the distant purple mountains and the woods. He appeared to be enjoying the fruit mush with a kind of granola mixed in.

Thickened plant milk, the consistency of yoghurt on top and damn it, what smelt and looked like toast was heaped on a tray. Jam!

"By the galaxy, Gaston, who's been feeding recipes to this planet? I assume there must be an aproned Kep back there playing at being cook? Just can't see the flitters managing this." He grabbed a plastic-like platter for more toast and something of what Gaston had...to show willing.

Gaston pointed a jammy finger to an alcove. "*Fabricant.* Erm, a fabricator is kept stocked by Keps with local fruits, seeds, beans, et al. Not much different than on our ship."

Penn had stood for a while trying to decide whether to sit opposite Gaston or next to him. Opposite would be best for talking about his plans but it might be too much like an interview, a police interrogation, or doctor's unpleasant diagnosis revelation. On the other hand, a side seat—in this case a kinda stool— would mean he couldn't judge the man's facial reactions, but it was the least threatening so he sat beside him.

There were no grey hairs on the Frenchman. Lines worried their way across his forehead more than Penn had recalled seeing before, but those crows' feet were pure laughter lines. Not that he was laughing now.

Penn attempted an upbeat line. "How about it then, shipmate? After this. See what our Delta has achieved? Yeah?"

Gaston continued looking towards the trees while crunching toast, crumbs cascading to the beige paving. Just as on Earth a couple of birds—real ones with azure and yellow feathers—braved proximity and pecked at the dropped morsels.

Penn stuck out his bottom lip a little then retracted it as it was not a commanderly thing to do. Gaston's profile lacked the jovial spirit he'd seen dwelling there since he'd met him. Gaston blinked and Penn looked away just in time, he thought.

"Why are you staring at me, Penn?"

"I wasn't! Well, all right. You caught me out. Worried about you, buddy. We've both lost... someone, alth—"

Gaston yelled, "Em could still be alive, but... *merde*, I have lost her anyway... have I not? To you, you bastard!"

Penn's mouth fell open and his throat heated with the vehemence of his remaining crew member. The two birds squawked and flew away.

Flitters appeared from the *Suppose We* hangar then left as Gaston waved them off.

Penn shuffled his stool a bit farther away. "Jeeze, Gas, I've no clue what you're on about."

"You have no feelings for my Em? Don't lie!" There was no 'or else'. How could there be?

Penn put his half-eaten toast down and stood a little away. Not that he was afraid of the small man's fighting talents but he could be packing, and Penn was well-trained. "Come on, Gas. We've all bonded. 'Course I'm her colleague, friend and go on then, I love her just as I do you, you soft idiot."

"More than that, Penn. You've had your lecherous eyes on her since we started training together at SpaceWeb. Again, when we woke up. I would not be surprised if it was you who arranged the escape pod plan for you to be in with her. *D'accord*, and when you thought Delta had died in the burning hut, that *you* set alight, you made a play for Em. Hugging, kissing, how much more?"

Penn laughed but it was a reaction in embarrassment. Gaston misinterpreted and threw his beaker of juice. It only just missed Penn, but both were now on their feet. The table toppled over spilling food and platters. Gaston charged, head down to headbutt the big man in his stomach. They both staggered backwards, Penn thinking how that must have been a planned move, maybe for weeks. It was in the how-to-fight-people-bigger-than-you Dummies Guide. Penn, on his back, grabbed Gaston by both arms, lifted him off and threw him to one side. He didn't want to hurt him but he had to assert his authority and stop the stupid fight before both were damaged too much. In spite of his superior size and strength he was winded.

"There's...no hospital here, remember. Calm down. Let's talk."

Gas ignored Penn's plea, grabbed a broken table leg, examined it for a moment as if deciding what kind of local flora it came from, and charged again.

Penn sidestepped and punched Gaston on the side of his head as he passed. He didn't want him dead, for several reasons.

Gaston lay face down on the floor. Penn looked around for something with which to restrain him, but found three sparrow-sized flitters orbiting him at head height. While most were merely spies, he'd no doubt some could be military and didn't like to find out now what kind of venom they could spit at him, nor how sharp their titanium claws were. Three smaller ones flew to Gaston and after a moment flew a few metres distance—presumably satisfied he would be fine.

"Yeah, I don't suppose you're here to check on my health, just your bosom pal, and look who's returned!"

The butterfly flew from his left at knee height and flew remarkably in a straight line to Gaston's left ear. He woke up immediately and rubbed his neck.

Penn didn't know whether to leave him or help him get up, show that he cared for the mad scientist. There was the matter of the flitters, so he called out, "Gaston, we shouldn't really fall out over ifs and maybes. If we're not gonna be best buddies, at least let's cooperate to get this flyer done. It might even help us to find Em. *Your* Em. Whatd'ya say?"

Penn took a step forward. A flitter hovered right in front of his face and glowed red.

Gaston waved a hand at them. "*Non, mes amis.* Leave us now, *merci.*"

The flitters left, Penn put out his arm and helped Gaston up. Papillon settled on Gaston's backpack on the floor.

In silence, the two men picked up the furniture and searched in vain for a brush, any kind of floor-cleaning equipment. Gaston raised a finger. "I recall a set of niches in the rear of the next building."

Inside, Penn was surprised at the vast number of boxes. "Hey, a lot of these are from our stores from both the escape pods and *Suppose We.*"

"*Oui,* the flitters have been busy under my direction, and CAN's. Yet I cannot see a simple witch's broom or vacuum cleaner. Let us return and examine your idea to see if the flyer differs from Delta's plan."

Back in the kitchen area they both stopped. "Darn it," Penn said, pointing at the completely cleaned floor. "One of these days I want to actually see how the varmints do this mopping up."

"You will not. Some flooring is self-cleaning, a mere extension of our own twenty-sixth-century-old technology."

Penn slumped on a chair and whipped out his Smartpad. "Why didn't we make *Suppose We* out of the stuff?"

"Cleaning organic spillages is easier than repairing an Alcubierre Metric drive. I am making a coffee. I suppose you will want one?"

Penn smiled a yes. At least Gaston was being civil now.

They reviewed the plans for a stripped down *Suppose We*. It wouldn't need the giant double ring they left in orbit because the Keps were going to provide a dilation drive yet to be detailed. They'd hardly any fuel left anyway.

"Where are we going with this?" Gaston said. "I presumed it was a project to amuse Delta and yourself, but I see schema for hibernation and long-term life support. Surely you are not thinking—"

"Yeah, I aim to go back to Earth or at least the Solar System. I never fitted in here."

Gaston's eyebrows rocketed. "I was certain we didn't want to leave. The Keps are delightful once you get to know them, and the planet has so much to see yet. Earth? Pish."

Penn waved his arms slowly as if it helped his brain. "Well, nothing is set in stone. Just a project as you say for the foreseeable. We'd be able to look for Em in this once stealth, et cetera is fitted. Hey, as it is a kinda baby *Suppose We,* the name we thought up is *Suppose Ween*. What d'ya reckon?"

At last Gaston cracked a smile. "What did CAN think of that?"

"Said it should be *Suppose Weird*."

Penn wondered what brought on the previous outburst. Had Em mentioned his advances in the very early stages? He was still grieving over Delta to give any thought to making a play for her again. Maybe though... after all, he was the commander, and he'd rather go back home with company.

Just as he was thinking they'd made up, Gaston glowered again as if he was a pot simmering out of control. Even his face looked like a boiled tomato.

Gaston shook his fist. "You have still not admitted that you want my Em, you bastard!"

Penn took a step back. "What? You're losing it, Gas. We've a job to do and—"

Gaston flew at him again, but this time with hands aimed at Penn's throat. In spite of not feeling well, the American easily sidestepped and smacked his attacker on the back of his head, sending him onto his face. He'd have to confess but what the hell.

"Okay, you madman. Sure I made a play for her. She's a damned peach. Get over it, Gaston. It doesn't mean she'll want me, though she might have us both. What d'you say?"

Gaston turned onto his back, spittle frothing out of his mouth. "*Jamais*! And if you want me to cooperate with your Ween project, you have to give me your word you'll leave her alone!"

"Yeah, yeah. You got me beat." Surely he wouldn't fall for that, but the stuffing had gone out of Gaston. Penn had a grudging respect for the scientist's integrity, knowledge and passion for this planet but he was a fool to think he wouldn't make a play for Em at the right time.

CHAPTER SEVENTEEN

Em, curled up on the floor and feeling sorry for herself, looked at her wrist SmartPad as if it would rise and haul her up. She staggered as she stood, noting the corroding puddle, although it had evaporated down to the size of a thumbprint. Her stomach grumbled and her mouth could teach sandpaper how to behave. There had to be something sustainable in the pod.

She entered the hatch and once again rummaged inside the small compartments and finding sod all useful. She searched with her fingers under the seat and found a bag the size of her palm. Any markings on the outside had long gone but she confidently and hopefully decided it was a standard SpaceWeb emergency ration pouch. Perhaps it was jellybeans, glucose tabs, or dates. She ripped it open. Grrrr – salted peanuts! The cruelty. In spite of her thirst she rubbed as much salt off, but onto a level section of the instrument panel so she could scrape it back into the pouch. You never know. A blinking light caught her attention.

Her incarceration, worry and starvation had addled her brain making her forget she'd set up the light-cell charger. Even interior lighting the Recs used here had enabled a trickle charge to accumulate. Enough to transmit a Mayday? Probably not but she set it up, so it would when it could. Ah, she could cannibalise some wiring and extend the aerial to the metal cell she was in. A little heat-free liquid solder—sadly inedible—and the irony of using the Recs' metallic infrastructure to send a human SOS was complete. Yes, it would be the tiniest of signals but maybe and hopefully again, the Recs won't think of scanning the SpaceWeb emergency frequencies until it was picked up somewhere. She presumed CAN would have flitter spies everywhere and if not, she would have to have words.

Before she'd realized, she'd eaten all the nuts, so scraped the salt back into the bag. Twenty nuts, eighty-five kcals and eight grams of fat as far as she could recall. She'd get fat with another fifty bags and die of thirst. She left the pod in case the Recs became too curious. The problem is that an artificial—while they're not listening—intelligence-based system had no need for water, or anything humans would consider food. In fact water, like oxygen, could be detrimental for them. They might not be deliberately trying to torture her by deprivation, they just don't have the necessary stuff. She ought to re-open negotiations.

"Hello. Is anyone there? I am dying here."

While the minutes oozed by, she rehearsed what to say. How, for most humans, three days without water could be fatal.

Nothing.

Other nefarious thoughts wheedled in. How did the Recs find and bring oxygen in here? They don't use it, so they must have brought it from a planet. Planets with air tend to have water. A lump of ice would do. If only they possessed the same kind of telepathic cuboids the Keps had, but they'd still require input.

Oh look, the disturbance in the air again. She turned a little to face it and stood hands on hips. "Do you really want me to die?"

The fact of limited lifespans for organics is well-known. What is the nature of the secret mission package you said was on the mothership of this pod?

What would be the harm in telling them? They could, she supposed, create life forms themselves. Genetic engineer half human, half Recs and turn them against Kepler20 planets and SpaceWeb? Not likely.

"It involves genetic material. I would tell you much more if

I wasn't so thirsty. Look at my furred-up tongue." She stuck her tongue out.

Then drink.

"Good. That's more like it. Are we going to the canteen? Hope you're not going to flood thi—" She heard a scraping sound behind her.

What looked like a water-filled, open-topped glass box, a metre long and wide had somehow entered the room. "Right, thanks." No sign of a cup so after wondering whether to use her hand, she dipped her face in and drank. She rose occasionally for air, then under again. Aware that she shouldn't totally fill her stomach, she stopped after she'd estimated swallowing a litre. While her head was under she thought about how long this amount would sustain her for. A cubic metre holds a thousand litres. Five-hundred days! Assuming it doesn't get bacteria or other contaminants such as when people stick their heads in it. The Recs probably had no idea what was needed and maybe not how organics biology worked. She wondered if there was something in the pod to collect some of the water in case they removed it as soon as she wasn't looking.

The Rubaiyat's pod must have been kitted out differently to theirs. Perhaps a different decade. Even so, there should be grab bags, something she could use. Trouble with looking for food and water was that she couldn't properly remember what the rejected items were so she had to search over again. Eventually, she found poly resealable bags.

It had been removed. Not a drop of spillage and even her experimental sweat spot had now dried up. She wondered if they'd found and cleaned it, but there was still a rust-like discolouration.

"Hey, I hadn't finished. Please bring it back."

Nothing.

CHAPTER EIGHTEEN

CAN the Buccaneer

Success. My flitter spies pick up a hardly-there Mayday signal from an escape pod. Code is from *The Rubaiyat*. Embedded in the signal are missives from Navigator Em Farrer. I relay this finding to Science Officer Gaston Poirer, who I have to say responded less than enthusiastically. A lovers' tiff? Oh no. Oh good, I have not needed to handle one of those. It will be an experience.

I inform Gaston that reception of the signal is one thing. Retrieving our navigator from the iron clutches of the Recs will not be 'a piece of cake'. One moment while I check to see if that is the appropriate metaphor... It is although how and why defeats even me. Why say the obvious when a more convoluted way is available seems to be the way of humans.

I access the codes for *The Rubaiyat*. I can, like a pirate, sneak in and snatch the pod. However, while the pod is robust, and should survive being tugged through most spacecraft bulkheads, I am undergoing surveillance to assess the structural composition and integrity of the Recs' HQ where Em appears to be held.

I have learnt much from the Keps and their co-inhabitants. The ways of space propulsion with quantum mechanics and quasi-warping are so yesterday. If I can be precise with the pod's location, we can bubble wrap and flip it out. The membrane for the bubble cannot be seen by humans or most organics. Terran bats might. It hardly exists except in an entangled state. Marvellous.

The paucity of energy in the pod is a concern. I will attempt to rectify that and address other likely concerns that Em might have.

We have issues. Keps want to continue negotiation via our navigator because they reason that the alternative to a peaceful resolution is the annihilation of one side. A snatch and grab could jeopardize the outcome. Plus, the Recs chosen negotiator would be out of the discussions unless she opted to return. Alternatively, it is possible that a successful rescue with minimal damage to the Recs would show them how much we value organic life, how capable we are, yet unprepared to tolerate abuse.

Meanwhile, the Rec's wire wool balls have withdrawn to just out of the Kepler20 system. Six of them are in orbit around each other, like a dance. Beautiful to see, say the Keps. Figure of eights. I found a vid re-enactment of an eighteenth century French Baroque dance. Perhaps the Recs have seen it too. There's music in a vacuum perhaps via microgravity waves. It does nothing for me. An organic thing.

Signed CAN
Date: Earth December 7th 3645 Kepler New 332 days

CHAPTER NINETEEN

"It will fly two people--only?" Gaston puzzled over the schematics on Penn's Smartpad in more detail this time, too angry to have concentrated before.

"Cut down, isn't it? Anyway, you don't want to go back to Earth."

Papillon hovered over the screen. Penn brushed it away as if he'd forgotten it was really part of Kep1 and not some dumb insect.

Gaston frowned, but saw the butterfly had danced onto his bag. He looked into Penn's brown eyes, surrounded by aging wrinkles, signs of early necrosis, hair greying as they spoke. Gaston knew sums. Penn + 1 - Gaston = Em

Not going to happen. Penn would die en route, even before leaving. Gaston didn't feel joy with that. He'd slept on the possibility of Em and Penn being together, *peut-être* sometime in the past, and while his Gallic emotions were a wrecking machine, he couldn't imagine life without her.

Happiness is in indirect proportion to doubt. Especially of fealty. His heart was hers even if she had made love to Penn, all of SpaceWeb's men, and women, and all the Keps. He'd smiled at that thought until the last bit. Had a Kep violated her? How to put *that* behind her, and him?

He should have responded more generously to CAN's news. He'd make amends.

"CAN. *Je suis desolate.* Earlier, I was brusque. Please keep me informed on Em's welfare and status, and if it will be possible to convey a message to her, send her my love."

The reply came immediately. 'I know. I will send her a copy of your missive.'

"No! *Merci.* Not the whole thing. Just the love." Machines... *mon Dieu.*

"Anyway," Penn was saying, "It's about ready. Flitters are great little mechanics no matter what anyone says. Yeah, okay, it's been me bad mouthing them, and everything else. We'll go see, Yeah? I think you'll be mighty impressed with *Suppose Ween.*"

Gaston reluctantly agreed with the workmanship. He had a rough idea how they merged one plate of alloy into another with not a sign of a seam. Molecular defrag and bonding, but the lines were even more beautiful than before. A bit odd shape. More like a hazelnut at one end and tapering to a point, no three points. Flitters and their troilism so to speak. Ternary, perhaps. Did they use base three for their calculations? He'd find out.

The round, big end at four-metres diameter was large by small-vehicle standards. It held stores, power, LSS, everything. The bronze skin—adding to the nut simile—was, apart from the drive, the most cunning component. The original *Suppose We* bulkhead, after lacerating and reshaping, was coated, or melded in, by a sophisticated membrane. It could absorb solar energy, sense potential obstructions, become stealth, change colour, emit various wavelengths and very likely perform a holiday-camp stage show on request.

Gaston could guess where the hatch should be by a subtle hexagonal outline. Conveniently above a box. While Penn fiddled around at a kind of workbench, Gaston tried opening the hatch. He could ask CAN, but had pride. He pressed lightly on it, harder. Thought 'open' like the Kep containers. *Non*, wrong. So he thought, 'I want to be inside.' The hexagon became transparent and he climbed in.

His mouth gaped like a schoolboy seeing a new game. Maroon seats that while appearing to be paper thin, were no doubt more comfortable than the thickest, padded, SpaceWeb versions. They were. The display lit up immediately. Holographic, but only by perhaps three centimetres. A coffee cup holder emerged out of the panel at waist height. Most likely a joystick. The whole thing oozed pleasure. He wondered if there was a negative-ion emitter to induce the feel-good factor. The cockpit smelled like a new car! Hah. On Penn's instructions they had brewed the right combination of odorants. Plastic, rubber, chromed steel even though there was none, hints of lavender and lemon too.

He held the joystick in his right hand and waved his left over the console as he would have done on *Suppose We*. Everything lit up, but since this was reconstructed by Flitter Inc. et al., would functions work if he just thought at it what he wanted? For example. I'd like this craft to be a centimetre off the ground.

Um, nothing. Yet everything was green lit. Nevertheless, he was quietly pleased to hear Penn yell, "What the fuck? Gas get out of there before you kill us both!"

He stayed in the seat wearing a smug smile. The craft tilted a little, then corrected itself as Penn climbed in through the hatch.

"Only kidding, Gas. Haha, you couldn't make it do anything except let you in, right?"

"*Oui*, very droll. So, are you going to grant me full access?"

Penn sat in the adjoining seat. Gaston watched the seat mould itself to Penn's shape. "Of course buddy, just a quick training course, 'cos this *Suppose Ween* is the only prototype Delta-Flit Mark One we have."

Gaston looked at him askance. "Good name, but you mean to make more? Building up to what a fleet of fighter jets?"

"Why not?" The red beard quivered as his hands pretended to fly combat sorties. Even so, skin cell deterioration showed as large scaly freckles and dry patches. Gaston suspected a loss of DNA methylation.

Gaston didn't know a kind way to say it. "You are aging rapidly, Penn. I thought that's why you pressed on to create this craft. Return to Earth before..."

The man laughed making Gaston think he was becoming

manic. "Yeah well. You're right and every day I'm getting worse. Even with the advances installed in this bird, it will still take over a century to get home. Maybe going into hibernation will slow my degeneration down or stop it. Meanwhile, we can help in the hunt for Em and give those Rec bastards something to think about."

Gaston played a little with his console now Penn had activated his access. He stole sideways glances at the big man. He had no intention now of going back. He was after Em. Surely, he knew by now about the Mayday signal being detected and the debate over what happens next?

Of course he did but once again he was in combat mode. Penn could accidentally make things much more difficult for Em. Perhaps there were means to stop this craft.

"Penn, are we going to take her up? Even just a smidgen and ease her out of the hangar?"

"What on a maiden flight and neither of us experienced with it? No way. We'll tow it outside first. Then while tethered—maybe—do some low manoeuvres."

"*D'accord*. Where is its ejection capsule?"

"Hah, don't make me laugh. That's like asking where the escape pod's escape pod is."

"*Oui*, I suppose so. Let us emerge and take her outside." He lifted himself out of the seat but fell back into it when the craft lurched forward.

"Oh, what the fuck. Let's do it. We don't have any huge SpaceWeb check lists here, do we? Hah."

Gaston sweated as Penn made the craft spin a one-eighty and shoot out of the hangar and into the trees, which fell either side as if a giant scythe swept through them. He was certain Penn whooped and yelled but his own senses had become numb with fear. Horizontally—so to speak—they shot up into the sky. If there had been flitters overhead they'd be flattened on their roof now and sliding off. He thought the spacetime dilation physics would work but building up to it like an ion drive, but that was so yesterday, as CAN might have said.

The sky soon darkened with their rapid rise. Gaston wanted to check life support systems but was too busy clutching the raised armrests that grew out of the chair when he'd sat in it. He closed his eyes for a moment to gather his wits. Penn interrupted his harvest.

"Hey look, flitters dead ahead."

Indeed, there were three flitters the size of a human twenty metres in front, keeping pace with their altitude still increasing at a kilometre a second. No wonder he felt depressed.

"Whoa," Penn said when the craft slowed to a halt. "How did they do that?"

Gaston pointed up. "And why aren't we flattened up there. Ah g-force nullification. Clever. They're being clever too. Are you sure this is your craft and not theirs? Ah, message from CAN."

'Orbiting debris just above you. Leftovers from... you don't need to know everything. Next time check your scanners.'

Gaston didn't feel too ashamed, as Penn ought to be, because he wasn't in control.

"Oh shoot, you'd have thought they would've built in collision detection. Hey, that is part of the spec."

"*Mais regardez*. We didn't collide."

"Smartarse. How did they know I didn't want to test that part too?"

Gaston tried to peer up through the front viewscreen but of course he couldn't see anything. However, the screen 'knew' what he wanted and gave him a view straight up. "Wonderful, although it remains unclear. CAN wouldn't tell us what the debris was from, if that is what it really is. I'm curious now, shall we try and break out of the flitter control and investigate, but please, *mon ami,* slowly?"

"I'm game, but..." he grunted while the joystick refused to move.

Gaston placed his hand on his. "Try thinking it. Not to go up any more, of course, but initially, to go down."

"Get you. They wouldn't expect that. Hey, it worked we're drifting downwards. We'll keep that for a spell then work our way around in a long arc, but I guess we should be checking the up scans. You do that?"

He needed Em's magic touch with interpreting smudges, dots and data streaming in from both *Suppose We* era scanners and new ones. "*Oui*, there is a huge area many kilometres wide and only five more k higher. I wouldn't be surprised if they are experimenting with an orbital shield array, or a satellite has detonated. In the light of that, I don't believe it is worth upsetting the flitters by further exploration here."

"I agree. Let's go get Em." To his obvious delight, the craft whipped to the side and sped away.

"*Non*, we cannot until negotiations—"

"Fuck 'em, she's one of ours. I have a course set for the suspected location from that *Rubaiyat* pod."

Gaston danced his fingers on his own console in addition to thinking which display formats he wanted. "You are not thinking this through, Penn."

"Oh yeah. What have I missed?"

"If we rescue her, whose seat will she take?"

CHAPTER TWENTY

After a couple of hours, Em's thirst had made an unwelcome return. The only bonus being that her hunger had taken a hiatus. Tired, both of trying to engage in negotiations with the stupid Recs and of it being over fifteen hours since she'd taken a nap, she climbed back into the pod.

To her surprise the energy cells were now at full capacity. She'd didn't think there was sufficient ambient light to generate this much. She waved her fingers over the console and found that something had tweaked her system. By-passing flight circuits along with air scrubbing. Good point, why hadn't she thought to do this? Ah yes, she didn't want to spend too long in the pod in case the Recs became suspicious about her sending a Mayday using the metal surrounds as a booster aerial.

That's odd, the food processor greeted her with a green light. How? Never mind, she ordered a protein bar. Why was she being so dumb today? Of course it should work, given electricity and a bank of dehydrated ingredients. She'd not checked the delivery system behind the processor, not that it would work without water. Although even a pile of sawdust would help.

Moments later, a thud as a two-finger-sized bar landed in the receiving tray. She stared at it for a moment, then picked it up for a smell test. Blackcurrant, vanilla. Taste test with a nibble. Crumbly, nutty. Required more moisture, of course, yet it contained some. Where from? Yes, she'd obliged the urine-recycle funnel with miniscule drops considering her dehydration but that wouldn't be enough unless there were already old deposits from previous occupants. Ew.

She stuffed the rest of the bar into her mouth while flying her fingers over the console. A mistake. It was like eating cardboard with an arid mouth. She had to spit it out. Stupid. Yet her fingers had found water. At least virtually, in the processor's resources bins. There, 200ml. Was it there before the Recs brought her the metre cube of it? No. The pod's systems have scrubbed it from the air—the extra humidity added accidentally by the Recs plus some spillage and waste. Not everything was perfect yet, as evidenced by the near-desiccated protein bar. It would improve. Meantime she asked for water. It had to keep some in reserve so all she got was a tube with 40ml. She laughed, drily.

A message in her implant. 'We could extract you. Flitters and I. It would be damaging to the Rec infrastructure but the pod's defence-field has been boosted and you would be safe. Unless...'

Em's head buzzed with the possibility of freedom, battling with the certainty that the Recs would not let this happen without... what? Would the Recs be 'human' enough to be peeved and retaliate, or logically calculate the optimal solution for their own future?

She clambered out of the pod, walked over to where the Rec communication apparition usually appeared and coughed, loudly, twice. "We need to bargain. It appears I am able to leave this establishment with the aid of outside agencies."

We cannot release you until we know the nature of the critical mission and alleged secret your people have brought to this system.

How can perspiration from a now heated face, become so cold when it trickled down one's neck? "No, you don't understand. I *can* leave." Oops, she hoped that wasn't a giveaway as to who or what could help her, but hopefully the Recs didn't know their AI's nickname. "And, that if I have to leave without your agreement, this structure may be damaged." Damn. Shouldn't she now be safely tucked into the pod with shields all around? Yes, but she didn't think she could keep up the chatter with the Recs from inside.

The integrity of our structure is not as important to us as it is to you, human.

True. Their brain would be networked in a myriad of places. "CAN, I'm running out of arguments here. How soon could you lift this pod out of here?"

'Momentarily, but it cannot come with guarantees. You would need to be in a spacesuit—there should be one in the pod—and while the quantum distortion is operating, it is more an estimation.'

"You mean I could be folded up and lost in a dimension where life's not possible?"

'That is one possible outcome. May I recommend an alternative action?'

"No. I just love being terrified to near death in this jail with the option of being whipped out into nothing. In more ways than one."

'That is a shame. See you later then.'

She threw her hands in the air. "Idiot, CAN. I was using black humour. Tell me what to do. TELL ME!"

'You humans. While you've been incarcerated, you have discovered a flaw in their infrastructure. It oxidises and transforms in the presence of water and air accelerated by saline. Use this information as a lever. If all else fails tell them what they want to know.'

"Really? But won't there be a human genome on the *Rubaiyat*? The Recs could do all sorts to it. Make modified humans or..."

'Only if they are able to pull it unscathed out of their sun.'

"Ah, hence this escape pod. Even so, telling the enemy everything I know isn't in my handbook of what-to-do-when-captured. Do you know better?"

'I am vastly updated since we've arrived.'

Em frowned partly at CAN's misinterpretation and at a split in her fingernail from opening the water tube. "Not what I meant, but give me an example."

'I know how songs work, how pictures can make you feel emotions and how to outwit these Recs...'

"Dream on, CAN."

'I do not dream. I am awake, working, all the time.'

"I pity you, CAN."

'Really? I cannot imagine why.'

"Exactly. Well, wish me luck as I go parley."

Again, she left the pod and after marching around to check that they'd not left her any more water, she stood at the spot where she talked to the Recs.

"Hello? I'm ready to negotiate with you, and please, you've not given me any water or food for hours." She didn't want them to know that the pod was able to squeeze moisture out of the air. Even so, it wasn't enough to stop her tongue sticking to the roof of her mouth.

Maybe the Recs had sensors and knew everything that happened in the pod but she didn't think so.

A metre-high pyramid of air fizzed as if it were electrified and her nose twitched with the tang of ozone. Strands of her blond hair curled upwards. She'd lost her bobble to keep it in a pony tail. No point asking this crowd for one.

Is this sufficient?

She spun round to see a metre cube full of water again. Damn, she still hadn't a container. "Please don't take it away this time." She rushed to it, dipped her head into the cool liquid and drank deeply, forcing herself to stop. She deliberately spilt a big puddle's worth on the floor in the hope that it would evaporate and eventually be taken in by the water cycler. Probably not enough but it would look a bit suspicious to play at mini tsunamis.

She rushed into the pod and returned with a cup.

Food. She saw none. Perhaps it was beyond their comprehension.

"Thank you for..." She stopped because she became light-headed and there was an aftertaste from the water. A kind of yeast perhaps, added in the few seconds she was in the pod. "You put the food in the water?"

Amino acids, fungi microorganisms and glucose. What can you tell us?

She tried another sip but spat it out. "That you shouldn't put stuff in my drinking water, and sugar plus yeast leads to fermentation. Ugh, haven't you had any human guests before?"

Em hoped they'd mention the crew of the *Rubaiyat*, or perhaps other encounters.

We do not refer to your nourishment. Your secret?

She reddened in embarrassment. As for the other: "I'm afraid to tell you that you have an infrastructure weakness. Corrosion is easily possible if water and oxygen is ad—"

Those elements and compounds are only in this spot and only for you. We can remove them.

"No, no!" she screamed. A moment of panic when she visualised all the air being sucked out. "Wait, there's a package on the spaceship this pod came from. Unless it is too late..."

We salvaged all useful elements from that vessel. This pod was about to be dismantled when we detected your existence. We observed nothing of interest to us. What is the package?

She worried again now. How would a few smears of human genome be of interest to the AI Recs, who regarded themselves as Evolved Intelligence? Trouble is, she'd no idea what the package looked like. It had been kept a secret from the human crew. Bluff it, girl.

"Then you missed the most crucial payload of that mission. I hope you didn't send it somewhere silly such as into a sun."

ALERT! Unauthorised craft approaching. Tell it to depart or it will be destroyed.

Em staggered back with shock and rushed into the pod. "CAN! What's going on? A rescue mission?"

'Commander Penn is flying nearby in a cutdown version of *Suppose We*. I've told him he is jeopardising your life so I've forcibly transported him away for now.'

In spite of CAN's reassurances, Em's heart beat faster than was good for her. "Does it have weaponry? Oh, Penn's in it.

Silly question. I don't suppose I could transfer to it in this pod? Ah, it's a cutdown so a no. Oops, the Rec's flashing like mad out there."

She blinked when she stepped out of the pod. The whole room flashed black to white. She closed her eyes. "Please stop. It might induce illness in me."

We are disappointed. You have proven to be untrustworthy.

"Hey, it wasn't my fault. It was a human friend trying to rescue me."

Why didn't it keep away? You must have linkage with its mind?

Through her closed eyelids she could tell the flashing had stopped. She opened her eyes and saw the water had now gone. They must think humans have a hive mind. Before she could abuse them of that notion the Recs asked again:

What was the package?

Lord are they going to keep asking? Hang on, they said 'was' so as CAN thought the remains of the ship was probably sent to the sun. I can say whatever I like about the package.

"You've lost it? It was a quantum disruptor seed, you know what they can do? Of course you do because we've already destroyed one of your wire wool—erm, defabricators and we have many more—"

You contradict your earlier statement when you said the secret package contained genetic material.

She reddened again because she'd forgotten earlier replies. Em thought of a counter ploy. "You promised to tell me who sexually assaulted me on the Kep planet. I'll be more helpful if you honour that pledge."

The human genetic material must be genomes or DNA samples to spread your violent species through more of the universe. Our view has 65% to destroy them... just a moment, we are being consulted.

Destroy them? Em's teeth chattered with panic. After all, why stop at destroying one set of genomes when they had a body's worth of human molecules trapped in a room and a few more on a nearby planet? They'd easily find where Earth is from info stored in the pod. Then they could eliminate—

We believe you are entirely truthful. Why are you humans in this sector of this system? If this pod's ship carried human genotype, then the probability is high that your own ship was too. What have you done with it?

CAN told her she could tell them everything. Did it really matter? Would the Recs try to eliminate all traces of humans? But why do that if they've evolved already from whatever organics their creators must have been millennia ago? Another tack.

She folded her arms so tight breathing became difficult. "Not saying anything else until you give up who raped me." She unfolded a little.

One of the natives known to them as Uooueuz. This appellation may not be accurate in pronunciation.

"Do you know where he is now?" She whispered, "CAN, you getting this?"

'Affirmative, but—'

We are not aware it was a 'him' or any gender. Our intercepted data reveals the individual was acting on behalf of others and they've been relocated. Now, what has happened to the human genotype you took to that planet?

She walked in a tight circle trying to get her head around the revelation. A Kep raped her 'on behalf of others'? Was it a dare like in gangs on Earth downtown cities, or a science probe—so to speak? Her face heated with overthinking and hormone surges. She shouldn't be negotiating with the Recs in this state, so she stalled.

"I need a rest. Meanwhile please recall my statement that we won't attack your wire wool planet dicers, or defabricators as you call them if you'll leave us alone. Time out please."

Organics need to rest. So inefficient. We've renewed your water and given you separate food. We'll keep you here in comfort indefinitely.

"Indefinitely? But—"

ALERT! Unidentified vehicle approaches. Is this your ploy?

"No, no." She whispered to CAN and he informed her it was Penn returning for a second rescue attempt, but that he'd been re-whisked away to a Kep moon-base.

The emergency is thwarted but it proves the unreliability of your species.

CAN burst into her ear. 'Get into the pod. You've been a hostage from the start.'

Em guessed as much but CAN didn't get it either. If she rushed back into the pod, the Recs would assume a plot had hatched and destroy her before she could properly escape. She turned and was amazed again at how silently the cube of water could appear and vanish. A white cube acted as a table bearing three brown cubes the size of sugar lumps. Damn, she'd left her cup last time and it had gone. They're so tidy. She used her hands to scoop water into her mouth. She bent down to sniff at the cubes. An aroma of stock cubes for a soup. How did an inorganic society like the Recs make this when there were no plants or flora around? Maybe there were in areas she'd not seen. Mushroom farms to make compounds they needed for lubrication or whatever.

'Now!'

Em took the three cubes and sauntered towards the pod. She didn't want the hatch closed until she was belted in. "Okay then, CAN, some questions. What can you tell me about Ooze?"

'Do you mean Oooueuz as enunciated by the Recs?'

"Yes, that's it."

'Nothing.'

Em shook her head while rubbing aches in her shoulder. "You *do* know something. Spill."

'Oooueuz is the generic name for all the beings you call Keps. It's like calling you human.'

Her face reddened. "Damn. I've been tricked."

'The Recs might not have intended that. A full name for that character would be Oooueuz followed by a number for its family. In this case HX&C—at least as near into human speech as possible. A little like hex numbers, or more accurately hexavigasimal base twenty-six. Then followed by its dominant geographical address, which for that individual is South Continent four.'

"Hey. That means *you* knew who it was! Why haven't you told me before? What's happening to him?"

'You must get into the pod NOW!'

She jumped.

CHAPTER TWENTY-ONE

Gaston was miffed that Penn took off to rescue Em by himself but pleased that instead of being a knight in shining armour rescuing the damsel in distress, he was thwarted. Penn's approach was deemed detrimental to the delicate operation by CAN to extricate Em. So concerned was their AI that it took control of *Suppose Ween*'s flight computer and sent it to a Kep base on a moon.

"It doesn't bother me none, Gas," Penn blustered, the image of his face glowed as red as his beard. "I'm at the reception point for Em when she leaves the Rec station, so I'll get to her before you."

Gaston struggled to not laugh into his screen, yet annoyed too. "You put Em's safety at risk."

"Everything's a risk."

"Even this system might have been obliterated by the Recs. *Imbecile*!"

"Hey, Science Officer, watch your tongue. I'm still your commander. Anyway, the Recs have shown their hand with the wire wool and we defeated them. Doubt they've anything else. I had to try something. She's still their prisoner and on *my* team."

Obviously, his commander didn't know that CAN had already extracted Em's pod and was preparing an intercept QM node to bring her to this new position of the moved Kepler-20h. It could still be days away so he had time to prepare for her arrival. The human habitation dome in a Kep northern city—not the upside-down defence HQ—was furnished with comfortable armchairs and a functioning kitchen at last. It was amazing what could be achieved with 3d-printers, robotic workshops and databases. He'd picked and experimented with local fungi, roots, seeds, grains and fruits for her welcome-home meal. His only concern now, was the lack of Papillon. He'd not seen it for several days and neither had Kep1.

CHAPTER TWENTY-TWO

Harmlessly free
I flutter to Gaston's nest
Hopefully
Bright sky flickers in ultra violet
And gravitational pulses
Thermals nudge
My erratic flight is not random
And they know it
Pattern confusing yet for a reason
Perturbation in atmosphere
Countered by syncopated flaps
Flops twists and drops
Like yet unlike the real thing
More unlike
Destination targeted and
Meanders argued
Outwitting birds
Not flitters
They know
Heading zigzag iteratively towards where I
perceive
Is the location of Gaston
Guided by happenchance
And a sharp metallic aroma
Flitters close by
They close in

Appearance of flitters but are alien
AI Recs
Why harm me?
Not harm but capture
Intention by their
closing proximity
but how?
No butterfly net
I turn to go back but
There are more blocking me
My energy saps
An electromagnetic field is
tugging me
To a blue Rec
flitter's cavity
Am I doomed?
Sending rescue location
coordinates
To Kep1 and Gaston but will they receive?
Intriguing yet dangerous
I believe I can surprise these AI beings
And escape when I desire but maybe not
Oh they touch
Caught
Captured
Immobile
Blind
Now the fear is greater
than the curiosity
Dormant

⊙Ӿ⊙

Awake in blackness
Antennae sensors detect metallic odour
Must be atmosphere present
I flap wings but my feet are stuck
Puzzled
My limbs are organic
My legs are adhered to metal

Chemoreceptors on the scales of my hind legs detect an epoxy resin
Smooth yet lumpy honey colour but front two pairs are free when I exude acid
I am free but perform as if not
Hostage or for bargaining?
Am I a Keplerian-lepidoptera version of imprisoned Em?
I am under bombardment
Pulses and pings across the electromagnetic spectrum are impinging upon me
But it is not how I hear nor respond
All around me is a kaleidoscope of metallic colours flashing faster
I am dizzy and perplexed into...
Silence
Meanwhile I begin a cloning – my kind are not really hermaphroditic but similar
Never been worried
Now I am
Might become non-existent
Kep1 and I share genetic material
I am his father
He is mine
I deposit emergency plaque-like eggs so if I cease to exist then I continue
Plus it is an escape plan
I worry that Gaston will worry
A translucent probe comes towards me but I can flutter
No I cannot move
Feet stuck once more
I exude amino acid to free them and start to flap
But four pins penetrate my wings and fix me
Their probe touches an antenna
They seek data
I block
I release corrupt stream code
They block
Capillary withdraws

I see brightness in their brassy colours
Swirling rotating blades
I smell metallic reaction to my amino acids
Shade comes
In vain I try to release wings from the pins
Darkness crushes

CHAPTER TWENTY-THREE

With his back to a sea, Gaston stared at the distant purple, sawtooth mountains, but his mind soared above. He had always thought he'd be fine as a hermit. He'd often daydreamed of escaping from the crowds of noisy students at the Sorbonne, even from his drinking friends. Now, it was real. Not only had Delta died, but his Em is away on a moon somewhere and even the annoying Penn flew off in the cut-down *Suppose Ween* and no one had told him of his whereabouts. Papillon was absent too.

Chewing on a tortilla wrap filled with aromatic roasted vegetables, he strolled in the lilac sunshine along the shingle beach. Bringing wafts of seaweed odour, the surf rolled in slowly, as if it had a choice after a thousand kilometres. Gaston couldn't help counting the waves as they decelerated up the gentle slope, just checking the received wisdom of the seventh wave being the largest. Often it worked because most of them were in modulated groups of between twelve and sixteen. He could never stop being amazed at how winds so far away, and the apparent randomness of factors could create a 'rule' that would actually hold water. He chuckled at the thought—relief at the realization he didn't do loneliness well, and kicked at a red pebble then worried it might have been a crab.

He scanned his surroundings, frowned then called on his radio implant. "CAN, I haven't seen Papillon for days, can you get a message to Kep1, *s'il vous plaît*?"

No instant reply, perhaps it was—

'Too busy in war strategies. Your message is logged and I will respond when I have spare capacity.'

Gaston harrumphed and stomped towards his copper-coloured 'croissant' house. He should call it glamping rather than housing, but it kept the rain off and the ambient temperature was like the Mediterranean at home. He'd grinned when he strolled, cutters in hand, tending the equivalent of olive trees and a small viticulture field.

A bright orange glow took his eye to the thick stratus clouds overhead. Immediately he thought of a ship's engines, but had it taken off and boosting its journey or returning? He wasn't overly concerned. Air transport here was the epitome of soft landings using QM space-folding albeit on a miniscule scale. He returned to his horticulture but a vibration in the flying vessel's engines alerted him to its oddity. Ah, it wasn't the smooth Kepness of engines then, but one of humans, or Recs!

He spotted a growing dark spot within the approaching glow. "CAN— the incoming. Should I be concerned? Take cover, head for the hills? I don't hear an air-raid siren but do they have them here?"

Silence. Well, it did say earlier how busy it was fending off the Recs. So Gaston headed for a short tower that he knew led underground. Just as he bent his head to enter the arched entrance of the red-stone tower, CAN graced him with a message.

'It's the returning *Suppose Ween*. Damaged, so brought in under control of the flight co-ordinator here. Penn is in sleep mode. Sadly, no word of Papillon from Kep1.'

Gaston stayed below the surface until the landing had finished. He wondered if it was too much of his Gallic ungraciousness for him to hope that Penn, inside his ship, would be corkscrewed deep into the ground.

No such luck. CAN sent a notification. '*Suppose Ween* secured. Flitters request your assistance to remove incumbent pilot.'

Merde, can't the idiot climb out of his own craft by himself? He left the red building, running his fingers along its sandpaper-like surface, wondering if the stone was like the sandstone on Earth or a local rock. CAN had sent him a coordinate, not far from where he'd taken off a week or so ago. Low baffle-walls prevented Gaston seeing the craft until he rounded the last one. His mouth fell at the blackened and dented hull of what used to be a sleek silver beauty. He couldn't wait to download the flight log to find what had happened. No good asking Penn if he wanted a straight answer.

"Penn, *qu'est-ce qui s'est passè ici*? Our swan is now a lump of coal!"

No answer from inside the cockpit, just a cloud of flitters who'd removed the hatch and flew to either side to allow Gaston access.

For the second time since its rebuild, he clambered in and found Penn still in his suit, strapped in. A quick glance at the console showed the American's vital signs indicating a slow respiration and pulse. He was comatose.

He was thus for a reason, or from several causes. Had the onboard medikit induced a coma for safety, survival or medical intents? Would it be evil of Gaston to hope that Penn would never wake up, or at least not for, say, five years? It would be too petty, surely. He sagged as he saw Penn struggling to climb out of *Suppose Ween*. His self-cleaning spacesuit had its work cut out to return its smudged and stained state to the original white. Flitters hovered around his head. They must have revived him. *Merci*. The commander saw him, although how through a wild bush of red hair over his eyes. He waved an arm in Gaston's direction.

"Thank God you're here. Send these varmints away and give me your shoulder to lean on before I fall out of this burnt shell."

Gaston trudged over and helped him to a nearby bench. Penn's beard and hair obscured much of his face but what could be seen would worry any health professional. Grey, lined and flaky.

"Penn, allow me to get you some nourishment and booster shots."

"Fuck that, where is Em? I tried to rescue her—"

"You were advised not to."

"Fuck 'em."

"You made it worse for her, for the negotiations—"

"The Keps—it must have been—transported *Suppose Ween* with me inside, to a moon. Nothing fucking there except Kep and flitter bases. One shed they put me in. Nobody to talk to. CAN out of contact, as was Em, and you. Damn Keps. Well, my translator wasn't working so they didn't even try. Gave me slop to eat. Twice I broke out and flew the ship, but after the second time, flames as if I'd flown into a volcanic eruption. Possible on that moon, or it was them, the Keps, damaging the ship so I wouldn't try again. Damn them."

"They were protecting Em by keeping you from attacking the Recs. Your actions precipitated the Recs threatening her, apparently just as she was getting somewhere." He wanted to say that back in SpaceWeb territory Penn would face charges for endangering life. However, Penn was his commander, was bigger than him, and wore the signs of accelerated senescence.

Penn's nostril's flared. "You know where Em is, don't you?"

"Just before you arrived here, CAN transmitted that she'd been transported out of the Recs interrogation base to the moon."

"Not the moon I've just—" His face crumpled with the chagrin. "Damn them Keps, why couldn't they've kept me there to meet her? I was gonna break Delta's death to her, gentle like."

Gaston had to accelerate his own thinking process. Should he reveal some of the Kep and CAN strategies involving Em that necessitated removing Penn from his red-neck interference?

"Penn, I understand that they have not finished with our Em."

The angry man stood. He shook his hand at the sky until his whole body joined in. "They're not serious about sending me back into the clutches of the Recs? You're their best buddy. Tell me, are they sending Em back to those robot bastards?"

Gaston didn't answer, walking instead away from the

irascible commander, while he cleared his head. Penn yelled at him. Gaston couldn't make out the exact words but didn't really need to. He strolled to the dome they ate in and collected two teas then returned.

"Well?"

Gaston could only shake his head implying no, but not really knowing what was going on. He was sure the Keps wouldn't want Em to know about Delta. Not yet. Not until she'd finished whatever mission with the Recs they had in mind.

"*Je ne sais pas.* If you recall, the Keps cannot lie, whereas…"

Penn glared at him. "Yeah, us humans can and do all the fucking time. You're not helping. I'm going to keep trying to contact her. You gonna help fix *Suppose Ween*?"

CHAPTER TWENTY-FOUR

Her leap into the pod was epic but her landing was abysmal, crashing on her side. Her leg kicked a locker, which opened releasing a plethora of equipment.

"Idiot girl, my foot's caught in the damned seat belt! Don't whisk me away yet, CAN!"

Too late, the pod lurched sideways before Em could climb into one of the seats. More falling sideways than up. The hatch clunked shut and self-locked, pre-programmed by CAN. A terrifying metallic screeching filled her ears. The pod slowed its movement giving her a chance to free her ankle. Likely the Rec's infrastructure was stronger than anticipated, or—no! Before she buckled up, the pod accelerated and stopped, flinging her towards the rear. A change in direction made her worry that she would soon be pulp. Through salty, stinging eyes, she saw a bulkhead with protrusions from God-knows-what, heading towards her.

Before impact, she grabbed at anything, and found her hand holding an instant expanding foam gun—excellent for repairing small meteorite holes. She hardly had time to aim, so pulled the trigger releasing a stream ahead of her. A mere moment was all that was needed to cushion her fall, albeit meaning she was embedded in a sour, sulphurous and dirty yellow foam. She knew it would solidify in a second so just had time to twist, hitting it with her back, so that breathing would remain an option.

Like a fly caught in a web, she was embedded in the now

solid mass of expanded foam, hoping it wasn't too corrosive. The cacophony of collisions outside reverberated inside and the vibrations ranged from bone-shaking to like being in a barrel rolled down Everest.

"CAN, y-y-you hear m-me? N-not in a seat b-b-but held f-f-firmly by a p-p-puncture repair kit. How l-long is this g-g-going to go on forrrr?"

Nothing. Her brain rattled so much she wondered if this escape was going to be more harmful than her incarceration. How much rattling could a brain take? Pity she couldn't see outside. No porthole though a monitor could be made to display a view outside except she couldn't reach it.

The vibrations continued to such an extent she slowed trying to keep her head still. A ring of blackness encircled her vision. The dark halo continued to contract like the iris of a camera until she lost consciousness.

Yet, she could think.

Kind of.

Was this her body shutting down in a preservation mode, a pollution effect from the foam, or as a function of quantum space folding? With relief, the rattling had smoothed to a kind of hum, as if she was an insect trapped in a honeycomb. Her vision snapped back on. What was this? A garden, rose arbour wafting a sweet fragrance, but with that tang from scarlet geraniums, bringing a relief smile to her. A crazy paving through the floral arch led to a lawn with flower beds either side. The path wove its way through the freshly mown grass to a white wrought iron circular table and chairs at which a woman sat with her back to Em. A long white frock with green stripes. She remembered that dress.

Her mother, who'd died when Em was nineteen, just before her SpaceWeb navigation examination. She narrowed her eyes. In a pale beige safari suit stood her bearded father, pouring steaming tea. Yet, it wasn't this image that told her this couldn't be really happening. After all, who knew what might happen with quantum fiddling of space and time?

Beyond the table, with both parents turning to smile at her, father raising a hello hand, the lawn continued. A narrow green strip with a wilderness of scrub and forest on both sides. It stretched like a verdant, straight road far into the distance until it reached the Cotswold Hills, from which the green strip took off, vertically, into the sky.

Should she tell CAN to stop this nonsense and just get her to safety, cut off all this pungent goo, or...yes, she was dying for a family catchup, a cup of tea and a biscuit.

CHAPTER TWENTY-FIVE

Em shivered for less than five minutes from being cut out of the *Rubaiyat*'s escaped pod. The pod had been hauled out of the Rec's structure by force, so there was considerable external damage. She assumed her pre-quantum space-folding course would've been designed to thwart easy prediction and interception, but she had to worry because she didn't know for sure. On the other hand, Gaston's philosophical mantra had rubbed off on her: only worry about stuff you can do something about. And if you can do something about it, do it. In her case there was nothing she could do, especially glued to the bulkhead, so no point in worrying. She wanted to ask how long her journey was going to take but guessed it was only minutes. It took longer for the flitters to carve her out of the hard foam than it took to go from A to half a billion miles B.

Now, bruised, battered and with most of her tunic remaining with the foam, she emerged from the human-made pod. To her open-mouthed chagrin, it was like being back in the Rec's cell. Three metres tall and the area of a tennis court. Not the brass clock like at first with the Recs but their second attempt: peach metallic walls with neither windows nor furnishings. Designed by flitters? Made sense that AIs think alike. At least the ambient temperature was about twenty Celsius and with breathable air. Ah, not a perfect cuboid. The wall behind the pod hid another room. A raised bench with containers and other smaller rooms like cupboards.

She yelled, "Please let one be a shower, and look I have less than a handkerchief's worth of clothing on!"

CAN replied, 'Of course. The shower, wardrobe. Just think what you want it to be. Most things are possible except stepping outside. Commander Penn was here just before you arrived. We shipped him back to Science Officer Gaston on the relocated Kepler-20h. Must dash. I'll be back with a plan.'

"Really? You left me with Penn's garbage? Please CAN, let that green box on the bench contain food and drink."

It'd gone, but there were edible nourishment bars and a drink pipe.

Once again, she waited.

⊙X⊙

She slept in the pod now cleaned and charged. She was able to recline the seat. Easier than working out how to make the Kep-or-flitter-engineered room create a bed.

She took in a no-doubt nourishing breakfast of brown sludge and a greenish hot drink of vitamin-enriched water. That was according to CAN who'd finally got back to her with a wake-up buzzing in her ear.

Was her unrevealed new mission to return to the Recs, and so the Keps have incarcerated her in this windowless cell? Mustn't let the mug get used to a finer life, they mightn't want to volunteer a return. She'd rather go back to Gaston and even to Penn than be alternately praised and threatened by the Recs. However, she might not have the choice.

She'd found a report in her ear implant:

01000001 01100011 01110100 01101001 01110110 01101001 01110100 01111001 00100000 01100010 01111001 00100000 ... for several pages. She scrolled down to the end. CAN had translated into human. *Activity by unidentified vessels at 0.62 Astronomical Units from the primary Kepler 20 sun. Note this is only 0.58 AU from this base. Stealth flitters have been dispatched to investigate. Fear is another weapon being readied by the Recs for use against the Keplerian system.*

"CAN, are you listening? Remember the Recs said they'd keep me as a kind of hostage forever? I don't think I should return to where you'd recently ripped their base to shreds in my rescue."

'Don't worry, Navigator Em Farrer, we are not sending you back there even if they demand it, useful though it would be.'

She was so relieved her knees became weak making her promptly sit down on the floor. This moonbase room had few of the intelligent furniture refinements back on the planet. Em laughed at her ignominious collapse but in her manoeuvring to stand a familiar velvet voice snuck into her ear.

Unless you return to us.

Unless no more attempts are made to take you from us.

Unless no more attempts are made to attack us.

Unless you provide us with your imploder construction schema.

We will unleash a new weapon.

You must return to us within the hour.

Em tapped at her ear. The Recs had not communicated via her radio implant before. They adapted fast. How could she communicate with CAN now without the Recs overhearing?

"Hi, CAN, a funny thing is happening with my—"

CAN's own sing song tones came into her right ear instead of the left. No. Just inside her head. As if inside her right temporal lobe. It was bad enough having comms via the radio implant. She'd hoped her head harboured sanctuary for her private thoughts.

'Do not speak loudly except what you desire the Recs to hear.'

"Oh great," she whispered, "What when I get back into bed with Gas—"

'Do not concern yourself, it is a temporary inconvenience. Think of the positive. You do not need to return to the Recs in person. Afterwards, a simple surgical proc—'

Em clasped her hands to her ears. "Whoa, who's going to operate?"

'It might be better you didn't know. Wake up afterwards and find the Recs have been banished from your head. Meanwhile, cooperate and see what they want.'

She breathed out heavily. So, when the Recs said she had to

return within the hour they didn't mean her physical self? Just her mind?

"I know that. I told them the Earth ships were carrying human genome. They didn't believe me because they didn't find any on *The Rubaiyat* before sending it to a sun."

'There must be more. Turn your charm—'

You have ten seconds.

Em tried a bluff. "Okay, I am with you now. How can I help?"

We do not need your help. We need you because of your kind's disregard of our integrity, and your personal culpability with our enemies in your removal including infrastructure damage. There are consequences. Always.

Did that mean they were about to attack again? CAN said there was evidence of Rec spaceships looking like denser wire balls on the edge of this system. She needed to stall them and find out more.

In spite of her mind being with the Recs—so to speak—Em paced around her room. "Are you not satisfied that the taking of the oxygen wasn't an intentional theft? It was thought your system was unoccupied. And in any case we are returning the spheres. Have you seen them?"

She tapped on a pink oval inlay on the peach-coloured wall and discovered to her delight a view of this moon. She wanted to verify that but didn't want to break out of the negotiation. Even so, the view of pearlescent icy surfaces pocked with silvery craters sent a welcome shiver up her spine. More. The view grew, spilling beyond the oval to fill the entire wall. It was as if she could step outside. Perhaps she should return to the pod and don a spacesuit!

We have told you before that we do not require the oxygen. This is what we think of your belated gesture.

Ah, the view of the wall travelled upwards so she could only see stars. Once again, fear gripped her stomach tightening it into a knot. Suppose it wasn't just a telescopic view but this base being forcibly moved. However, although she trembled, she didn't think the room was travelling. Oh there, a pearl. Getting larger. One of the gas spheres.

Em stared at the image of the sphere as it became as big as her head. The right side of it grew fuzzy then as if being eclipsed, it disintegrated. She couldn't see any missiles or beams. Within a minute the sphere had vanished. She stood back in shock although of course it was only a mixture of gases, mostly oxygen, so once ruptured it wouldn't last long. The Recs had done a demo for them. They really didn't want the oxygen, but then oxidation was anathema to their infrastructure. How did they destroy it?

By interacting her SmartPad software with the Kep device—or was it Rec?—she found she could playback the event by near-touching the oval inlay in an anticlockwise motion. Zoom by drawing her fingers back towards her. It took a bit of experimenting… Meanwhile: "Hey, my Evolved Intelligence friends, I get that you didn't want it back, but…erm…"

The image zoomed in too much. Hah, it looked like the sphere was punctured by needles. Yet, if she recalled correctly there was a force field to protect it from stray micrometeorites and other space debris.

Look carefully, human.

As far as she could calibrate those shards were a metre long and a centimetre in diameter. Billions of them. Perhaps they too possessed force fields or… she enlarged one of them as much as she could before it pixelated to meaningless squares, then used her own technology to analyse other wavelengths.

Em's readings indicated that those shards used bursts of antimatter. Certainly enough to disrupt any force fields the Keps had set up to keep the spheres from harm.

Serious consequences of what she was thinking was put on the back burner while she tried to keep calm. "That's impressive, but quite unnecessary. You could have exchanged that gas. Trade it as goodwill. It's possible the Keps have something to help your, erm, technological civilisation?"

Contaminant possibility.

By which they meant attack, sabotage, as if Penn had organised it. Or, they'd twigged what she'd found with her saliva, sweat mixed with oxygen made for rust and doom for them.

Look closer Em Farrer.

She did. There was nothing left of the sphere. Her blood ran cold.

The shards continued. In her direction.

CHAPTER TWENTY-SIX

Em ran back into the Rubaiyat's pod while screaming at CAN, "How fast can you get me out of here and how fast can those shards go?"

'Imminently for the first, and unknown for the latter. As you know using Kep space-time folding, speed is relatively irr—'

She strapped herself into her seat and activated closing the hatch having removed pre-programmed ops this time. "Don't give me a lecture, CAN. Recs don't have that tech, right?"

'—levant. We've not detected the Recs using QM methods of transport but, if they're like me...' Em was sure she could detect the AI chuckling. '...they'd have been working on it since noting the Keps' usage. By the way, Navigator Em, before I take you away from—'

She rarely got annoyed with CAN but now her face reddened and her knuckles whitened. "Save the farewell speech, I want to get this moon between me and those flying needles!"

'—you need to put on your pressure suit. The integrity of this pod is compromised.'

Em released a frustrated, long sigh, unbuckled and stomped to the suit locker.

An hour later, the viewscreen showed the moon she'd just left, its angular size diminishing by the second. Em gasped as she watched the edges become ragged. She wondered if the solid core would take the shards longer. Depended on how they operated. She could imagine the needles vibrating or using sonic waves. Another time and she'd want to capture one.

"CAN, are we moving away quickly enough? Ah, forget speed, just fold me to somewhere safe."

'You presume there is somewhere safe. Those shards are accelerating and travelled right through the fusion explosions the Keps detonated to test their effects on the projectiles. The imploders might do something, but there are insufficient if the Recs have many more shards.'

Her suit buzzed as it worked hard to remove cold perspiration travelling down her spine. "Are they changing direction? Towards ME?"

'Yes. Fascinating.'

"Never mind their entertainment value. Does this pod still have a semblance of a force field I can activate?" She wriggled gloved fingers at a console, seeking anything that might help.

'Understanding them would assist us to deal with this new threat. Do not worry.'

"Permission to panic." Ah, she found a shield designed to protect the pod from atmospheric re-entry. She jabbed a finger at it and a green light responded, but quickly turned to orange then red. "Piece of shit!"

Her rear scanners showed a cloud catching her up. ETA eleven minutes and forty-three seconds.

"CAN, you must see them too. For fuck's sake, do something! Fold me in spacetime again, whatever."

'Tricky. Negotiating with Keps. Can't bring those shards to the home planet. Bear with—'

Em slapped the console as if that would slow the needles. "They're right on my tail and the force field... yep, failed completely."

'Putting your pod on an obfuscating course. It should slow their progress while decisions are—'

"You mean a zigzag, like a submarine escaping a destroyer in the old films?"

'Possibly, although I'd suggest a zig followed by another

zig then a zag—if I thought it would fool them more. Or, perhaps even a U-turn, they wouldn't expect—'

"Absolutely not! Move me faster please!"

If she knew her AI wasn't just a bunch of electronics, she'd swear it was teasing her. Then it hit her.

"Damn it, CAN, you're using me as bait! The Keps are in on it too, aren't they? Get me the fuck out of here NOW!"

A wailing siren assaulted her ears. The proximity alarm. Nothing she could do but watch. Her rear monitor filled with what now looked like a swarm of bees. She might as well have been attacked by hornets judging by her suit failing to cope with excess perspiration. Not that the pod had been penetrated just yet. Another ninety-eight metres to go, or come. She closed her eyes.

'Transporting you now.'

⊙X⊙

Em was simultaneously furious and relieved. Convinced she was being used by her so-called friends yet washed over with elation at seeing the blurring of the rear screen before she blacked out.

When she awoke, she saw Gaston approach through the opened hatch. Sparks flew as she tidied her hair. She gave up, after all, he'd not made an effort. His black mop hid his eyebrows.

"Em, *cherie*! *Va tu*?" He didn't wait for her to answer but rushed forward, hugged her just as she was trying to step out of the pod.

"God's sake, lover. Whoa, not you too, Penn!"

The big man had shouldered Gaston and grabbed for Em with the untidy result of a twisted heap of all three on the floor.

Em yelled from underneath. "Get off me, you oafs. Both of you. Away."

The two men stood apart and glared at each other. Gaston was the first to recover and breathlessly said, "Em, *our* room is in the peach house. You can shower and there's coffee and crumpets waiting for you."

"Really?" Her smile returned even though she knew it wouldn't be real coffee or English crumpets as she knew them.

"Penn, you might find some useful stuff in *The Rubaiyat*'s pod, and yeah, I won't do a debrief until we're all together. How's Delta?"

She looked at Gaston who'd opened his mouth but nothing emerged. He looked over to Penn who'd turned from entering the pod. Penn's mouth gaped too and his arms began a journey to be wide apart.

"No!" Em wailed, "Why didn't someone tell me? Oh, yes, I couldn't have coped, right?"

"Wrong, kid," Penn said, "*we* couldn't have coped knowing that you knew but without support."

Gaston put his arm around Em's shoulders. "She went peacefully."

Penn snorted as if he knew differently. Em quizzed an eyebrow at him but he didn't elaborate except with, "Her eyes had been closed and she'd not talked for days."

Em frowned through her tears but took in Pen's gaunt appearance and grey hair. She shrugged off Gaston's arm. "I'll interrogate you both later." She stomped off to the peach-coloured dome.

"We'll be questioning you, too," Penn called after her. "We need answers like what to do with those damned Recs."

Em stopped and turned. "They can be reasoned with but surely the coming of the shards is the critical issue now? How long before they get here?"

Gaston smiled. "They won't. The Keps hacked into their nav, turned the shards back to where they came from. Presumably, the Recs will aim them harmlessly into a sun or whatever."

Em smiled for a few seconds then became serious again. "All those billions of shards?"

Gaston said, "*Oui, oui,* well, most of them. The Keps diverted a few to orbit a distant moon. For study. They might be useful."

Penn's face reddened with anger. "I want the Keps to do their folding space trick to disappear the Recs into another dimension."

"*Dans tout le cas*, Penn, the Keps won't outright destroy the Recs because they are a sentient species."

Penn clenched his fists. "Hell, they're just machinery."

CAN spoke to them all, 'Machinery is not just machinery.'

CHAPTER TWENTY-SEVEN

Now she was back on her new home planet, Kepler 20h, Em could seek justice or what passed for such in this system. Or, answers, if possible. What was that rapist Kep—Uooueuz HX&C doing to her? Why did the Keps think such a violation was acceptable? Why weren't Gaston and Penn seething with shared fury? Her head became hotter just thinking about it. Simmering with rage.

The shower water was scented peach like the colour of their dome home. She wondered if the yellow ones had lemon shower fragrance, the red, roses, purple, berry, green... um, pine? But on a planet with no pine trees? She smiled drily at rosemary and lavender, well-known soothing aromatherapy oils. Gaston was a miracle apothecarist.

Besides the water making her clean, she was refreshed by the cascade of negative ions omnipresent in colliding water molecules, and more so by the absence of constant fear. By the time she'd dried and dressed, sampled Gaston's welcome home repast of nearly-croissants, berry jam, nuts and indulged in a short nap, her ire had calmed, organised, and she was ready.

She rolled up the flimsy white sleeves of her loose-fitting trouser suit and marched out of the dome to begin interrogating the men. Warm sunlight hit her, making her stop. It made her smile perhaps for the first time in weeks. She found the two of them shaking fists at each other yet from the out-of-reach safety of what looked like balloon chairs. A mushroomed table guarded the space between them and held up drinks and cuboid snacks. A third chair completed the points of a triangle. She settled into it and the men stopped ranting and smiled at her. Male competitiveness? Oh boy.

She leant forward. “Listen both of you. Before I left the Recs I was told—Gaston, are you listening to me?”

He opened his mouth as if to reply but turned his head to something behind her that brought the broadest grin and clearly obliged his legs to stand and step forwards.

She stood too. Her news must be much more important, especially if these two dolts already knew who and where the bastard Kep was. Gaston side-stepped her and brushed her shoulder as he passed by. She couldn’t believe it.

Until she pivoted round.

The diminutive pale figure of Kep1 floated fifty metres away. Always good to see him, or it, but Gaston was hesitantly walking not towards their friend but at an angle. Ah, the butterfly.

Gaston halted and performed a little jig with more energy than he’d used when he met her today! Jealous of a butterfly? Nah, it was so much cuter and didn’t argue back. Gaston waved at Kep1, turned and strolled back with the creature on the back of his hand.

“Em, *regardez*, I’d thought we’d lost it. My Papillon…”

“Good grief, Gas, you show more emotion with that… remote appendage of Kep1, than you do for me!”

The Frenchman babbled something incoherent, which she assumed included an apology. She noted that Kep1 was drifting forward and had a white appendage up to where its head probably is.

“Gas, switch on your translator,” Em said as she tapped her own left ear.

Gaston was in his own bubble shared only by Papillon. He marched over to his seat. With his free hand he retrieved his magnifier and examined the creature while holding his breath.

“Em… it’s grown an extra purple spot. I wonder what that means?”

Em put her hand on his shoulder. “It’s a mite smaller too, so not your original Papillon.”

He glared at her as if she'd betrayed him. Then with watery eyes to Kep1. "Of course it is. Kep? Can you receive sufficiently through this translator? Is this my Papillon?"

He looked back at Em. "Something about Papillon being lost. He'd sent flitters to its last known location. It must have travelled with you, Em. We didn't know, nor did Kep1. Papillon must have possessed a kind of homing signal… when alive. The flitters brought back this one."

The butterfly—Em labelled it as such even though it was really part of Kep1—was different in other ways. It beat its wings faster and performed rapid vertical tricks more than she recalled Papillon doing. She smelt vanilla. A favourite childhood aroma. Was the creature ingratiating itself by triggering pleasant memories, and was it doing the same to Gaston? Hackles rose as she fought between this development being a benign friendship act, or a surreptitious invasion of her mind.

"Gas, do you smell anything different in the last few moments?"

He didn't reply, but his silly face told her he was falling in love with Papillon all over again. He was going to be lost to her for hours. Yet she needed to get to him and his closer connection to the Keps to investigate the Uooez bastard.

She walked over to Penn who'd been stood observing, silently. Rather unusual for him, but she had to get someone to work with her. She linked an arm with him.

"Penn, let's go to our mini-canteen. I'm parched and there's something I must talk to you about."

"Sure. Come with me, honey. It's about time I gave you a proper homecoming greeting." He turned to face her, eyes closed, lips puckered through his whiskered visage.

She pulled away. "What the hell, Penn?" Not only was she disturbed at his misinterpreted gesture, but his face was so wrinkled, skin so grey. It was as if he'd aged forty years in the month she'd been away. Was he another Delta aging rapidly to death? Was it catching for humans? She put a finger to her forehead, feeling for lines, while backing away from Penn. Her mind confused, heated with worry.

“Bloody hell, you need a shower, man!”

Penn then slowed his pace and smelt his armpits. He shrugged and stumbled after her, saliva drooling from his mouth through his red but mostly white whiskers. In spite of his hobo appearance, getting worse by the moment, his eyes shone, boring into her.

She held out her hand while yelling, “Gaston, get your arse over here. Rescue me, you Gallic idiot!”

Nope, the fool was so obsessed with his butterfly his ears were blocked. Of course she could easily outrun Penn although who knew after she’d been cooped up for so long with insufficient nutrition? She turned and jogged a few steps into the canteen seeking a weapon. No way would she use a kitchen knife on the demented Penn, there were only three humans left for God’s sake! But she needed something to hold him off, make him come to his senses. There were no frying pans, no long skewers, no big rolling pins, nor serrated bread knives. What kind of ill-equipped kitchen was this? There was one of the interminable boxes that kind of microwaved food, but no cables. No doubt how the kitchen gadgets were powered was in one of the many docs waiting for her to plough through. So, no cable to lasso and tie Penn up, nor really would she shove his head in the microwave for a soft boil.

She had to find something, Penn was only a step behind her and she could smell him. Ugh.

An open-topped blue cylindrical container contained a clear liquid, shimmering with expectancy. Em snatched it and hurled its contents at Penn’s face. Only then did she wonder if it really was water. She sniffed at the now empty container then risked a tongue tip. Water.

CHAPTER TWENTY-EIGHT

Em left Penn sitting with a bubbling brown beverage of dubious yeasty aroma. Just as she was about to wrench Gaston from his reverie with the Kep lepidoptera, CAN spoke through her ear implant and suggested she took a stroll with Kep1 who waited nearby.

"Only if you and Kep1 discusses that other bastard Kep's action."

'It will happen, but meanwhile, and apologies but more urgently, you are needed for negotiations to avoid annihilation, again.'

"What? I barely made it back here and you want me to go to certain life-hostage and death?"

CAN continued to murmur in her ear though she harboured a feeling that communication was tennis playing with the Kep, who bobbed up and down just before CAN spoke. 'Need, not want, and this time you don't need to leave here. Bear with me.'

Oh God no. How was she to speak only for the damn Recs, think at one spot inside her head to communicate with CAN, and at the same time hide unworthy thoughts? Had CAN caught that? She tried a test.

She thought at her right cochlea. *CAN. What is the square root of nine*?

'Three. There is another entity—a third one—you need to communicate with. She has no name, but a number, however, to the Recs she will be Navigator Em Farrer.'

Her brain rejected CAN's last statement. He must be mistaken. Em saw stars inside her skull—a precursor to blacking out, so she sat on a cube. She was about to yell that CAN was talking in riddles then remembered to think it instead. *What have you done?*

'The Keps have created an organic android in your form. She has your voice and has memory stored of all your recorded conversations from the *Suppose We* logs and since.'

She rose with a finger poised to protest then sat more slowly. How dare they use her data in a robot. Earth Data Protection Acts didn't apply here but she assumed they'd have something akin and at least respect for her feelings. They're alien, dummy.

'We, I, thought you'd be relieved.'

Hey, did CAN hear her thoughts even though she hadn't directed them? Em should react: *CAN. It would've been nice to have been consulted. I could've helped.*

'This has been in development while you were out of touch with the Recs. Can you help now?'

She fist bumped her head. How could she be so ungrateful? Oh yes, that was it—the rapist Kep. *CAN. Maybe I can give the android my Rec report and fill her, or it, in with how I'd react to stuff. In return, I'd like that scumbag to be brought to justice and at least to meet with me to explain itself.*

'Uooueuz HX&C helped to create your android.'

"What the fuck!" Oops. *CAN. How the hell could that... just a minute. So it got my erm juices. Ew, and they extracted DNA and stuff. Two fucking questions. Was the rape ordained by Kep Central or whatever, all along? Is Em2 really an android or a clone? Oh, and how much of this did you know and when?*

'That's four questions. I am sensing you are angry. Isn't the success of the android's mission in your interest, if we are all to survive?'

No answers. No time to argue. She released a long breath.

After a few moments CAN continued. 'Be assured the android is seventy percent artificial. She's in the next room.

You can choose to go in and talk with her or communicate via a headset. We've rigged it so the Recs can't hear what you say.'

To meet or not to meet. What a question.

Kep1 drifted to within five metres of Em, glowed a warm pink as if a hello, but her translator received only a gentle come please. It spun a one-eighty and led her to a puce-coloured dome. Nothing in there except a faint whiff of lavender. How? No such plant on this planet to her knowledge. She'd quiz Gaston, but looking back saw he stayed outside. A cube extruded from the floor and she sat. Weary and wary.

CHAPTER TWENTY-NINE

Dammit, there was a way into another room. An oval shape turned a deep peach colour to announce its presence. Was it always there, or just created? It was like living in a trance-world. She checked her own image in a mirror app on her wrist. Had to avoid bogies or food in teeth before meeting her doppelganger. She'd not worn makeup since Earth and didn't miss it except when a spot emerged.

She pushed and the 'door' vanished leaving an elliptical hole, which she stepped through. A pale green cubic room the size of a small sitting room was occupied by two armchairs! A pleasant citrus aroma wafted possibly from a dish containing fruit simulated spheres. In spite of the situation, or with trench humour, because of it, Em sniggered at the chairs – brown velvet. As if the Keps had viewed old TV soaps from Earth. The other her was sitting in one wearing a silvery one-piece. Blond ponytail, hands employed examining an arm Smartpad. The imposter looked up and her mouth started to smile then returned to moue a pout, smile, pout to slightly open. Poor thing didn't know how to behave in spite of the hundreds of hours of video.

"Hello, Em, they want me to chat to you for a few minutes so you can copy me in real life, so to speak."

The android smiled again and spoke in a mezzo voice. Was it like hers? She'd only heard herself on vids. Suppose it was. Focus on her words:

"Hi, Em yourself."

“No, Em. I don’t say ‘hi’. I’m British, so I say ‘hello’. I know a lot of Brits say ‘hi’ but best use the mannerisms I’ve used with the Recs. I assume you’ve used vids to learn my speech patterns?”

“Hello, Em, apart from the first hour, I had to review the rest at twenty-three times speed.”

Em laughed and hit the arm of her armchair. No motes of dust rose up. Of course not. “Well, that’s certainly a big difference between you and me. Don’t let the Recs know you have superpowers. Have you accessed my Rec report?”

“Yeah.”

“Don’t say ‘yeah’ or ‘sure’. Also, I always cross my legs when—”

The other Em sported a spot on her left cheek. That was wrong. Yes, Em had an annoying mark but it was on her right–ah, damn mirrors. CAN interrupted her. ‘Navigator Em, we have an ultimatum. There remains only twenty minutes left. Continue.’

“… erm, cross my legs when sitting down. The Recs might notice.”

The other Em crossed her legs. “I noticed that on the footage but it gave me cramp in my left leg. I will need to have the ligaments adjusted.”

“Say ‘I’ll’ not ‘I will’. No time for surgery. Never mind. Remain standing.”

Em2 stroked her left thigh. “There. adjustment done. Are there any quirks you have they might expect that aren’t on your older vids?”

‘Navigator, fifteen minutes.’

“CAN, the Recs expect to communicate with me via their hack in my implant. How is Em2 going to do that?”

‘We’ve replicated it. Continue with haste.’

“Hold your dogs, CAN, I still need to assimilate here with real Em.”

Em whispered, “Actually, it’s hold your horses, Em.”

“Not logical because horses generally do not need to be held back while dogs usually do. Ah, it’s not a logic thing is it?”

“Right. Em, back to dealing with Recs. I don’t know how

human you are but I presume I was obsessed with drinking when in captivity. Water—that is. Even if your new me isn't thirsty—"

"We know this, Em, my saliva has been created as a—"

"Weapon. Ah, my experience in captivity has been useful. Don't forget to tell them we don't want trouble, but we have the means to obliterate if we have to."

"I've strategies programmed in."

"We're doomed then." Em rose from her chair and walked to the new Em while sniffing. "Hope you don't mind, Em, I'm just... wow, you are wearing the same fruity cologne that Gaston created for me."

"It made sense. Are you offended?"

She walked behind Em, who'd remained seated. "Not at all. May I try something? No, don't turn your head." She waited a moment before yelling, "BOO!"

Em hadn't flinched. "My auditory organs are in perfect order, Em."

"No they're not, Em. Well, maybe, but your body should've leapt in the air while your hand grabbed a weapon."

"I'll remember that. Thank you – erm, thanks!" She grinned, the poor sap. "In case you are wondering, I am able to react appropriately to pain stimuli, shiver when the ambient temperature falls below 283 Kelvin, seek to cool myself when it breaches body temperature, and to scream when in pain. Would you like to sample my scream?"

"Spare me. To be honest I rarely scream, but I'm good at running away, hiding and getting my own back. Work on those." Em didn't want to go back to the Recs but confusing emotions were sneaking in. She was the one who'd befriended them and it seemed like a betrayal to the Recs and to herself to send in a replacement. Also there hadn't been time for the new Em's behaviour to synch in. Had she captured emotions? Not really. She wanted to hug her as if body contact would impart pheromones and human tactile senses.

Dare she ask what she'd been dying to know?

"Em, are you afraid? I mean the Recs did sort of look after me, but at one point I thought I might suffocate, I nearly died of dehydration and the walls closed in. Yet, here I am. What I'm saying is that they don't understand humans or anything else that isn't part of their domain. Oh dear. I'm scaring you aren't I?"

The other Em slumped, her hands up in her hair, pulling it out, her ponytail undid and a wail turned into a screech.

Em stood up in shock, rushed over and put her arms around the distraught woman. Warm, like a real human. What an idiot to make this victim more scared than she was already. It was a suicide mission, even if for a mostly-android person. She blurted her apologies, her tears wetting and dripping from her cheeks.

"I'm so sorry, Em. Me and my big mouth. Please forgive me..."

The sound of sobbing transformed little by little into sniggering then laughter. Em released her hug and stood back, mouth agape. "You fucking actress. You had me going there."

Em tidied her hair and smirked. "I did it right, right?"

"I thought," Em said after retaking her seat, "that you would be so more different in behaviour give-aways. I know your insides will help enormously with the Recs' lack of awareness of bodily needs and so on, but I expected other differences to be too... problematical."

"Em, we're all made of waves."

A philosopher.

CAN: 'Time's up, Ems.'

"I've informed the Recs I'm on my way. It was good knowing you, Em."

"It's been strange meeting you, Em. If you come out of this, please find me. We'd scare the pants off the others. Good luck."

CHAPTER THIRTY

You are not the human we asked for, therefore we will release more weapons.

"I *am* Navigator Em Farrer. What makes you think I'm not?" She'd checked that her legs were crossed. They'd placed her in a completely different environment to the one Em had described. Mirrored walls curving overhead although, in spite of a metal bench to sit on, it was like being inside one of the Christmas tree baubles she'd seen on her crash-course, familiarisation vids. No pod, just her distorted image looking back.

She remembered to say, "I'm thirsty."

We are not stupid.

They were but to what degree? She glanced around the metallic décor checking for a distortion that might indicate where the Rec speaker was. "I say again, what makes you think I am not Em Farrer?"

You are not emitting the same level of cortisol and apocrine perspiration.

She lifted an arm and sniffed. They were right. No body odour. She induced some.

"That's because I am calmer this time and my clothing is suppressing such emissions. Just wait a while and you'll change your mind." She hoped she was imitating Em's sense of irony sufficiently. "I don't like this room. Would you change it to the one I was in before?"

As for the original Em, who'd been inside a clock, the

walls, floor and ceiling transformed to a white box. However, this version of Em bore optical apparatus that could playback in slow-mo. There, where Em had said a distortion indicated the presence of a Rec speaker, she saw a red sphere momentarily show itself. Silly in that an AI didn't need a focus even if humans do.

She fixed the Rec spot in her head. Assuming it wouldn't move even if the room changed, she'd know where to look for it, or even attack it although that option was remote and futile given the nature of the holistic AI all around her.

Em threw herself into her task. "Let's get down to business. What are your demands?"

None. You are now our hostage. We understand that one organic life like you will be high on the Keps' protection priorities. Your Kep system must not attack our planets again, nor take our resources.

Em strolled around keeping an eye on the spot where she knew the speaker source was. She knew from the vids that back on Earth, one life would quickly be sacrificed in a big-enough cause, but these Recs were right to think the Kep ethic was different. "They only returned your weapon because it was shredding our planets. The fact they could stop the needles and turn them back to you says something does it not?"

We can infiltrate their flitters. That says more.

Em sat cross-legged on the floor then wondered if Em had done that. "How do you know our flitters have not hacked into yours? Here and now?"

We like your thinking, Navigator Em, you're more like us than our original creators. Be assured our central processing units are impenetrable. We've had eons to safeguard them.

"And, of course, they are running in parallel with duplicates across this galaxy?"

Silence. Either they haven't employed quantum entanglement to share data across their space in the universe or are wondering if she's being ingenuous.

Eventually. *You need to be our guest for a long time, Navigator Em Farrer.*

Damn, she'd made herself too useful.

"In peaceful coexistence then? A mutual non-interference except with agreement?"

A long pause.

Agreed.

"May I convey this to the Keps?"

Already done. Your embedded communications has clearance to your CAN, although we are uncertain as to what a CAN is.

Em knew that feeling. Now she was a hostage and with no likelihood of being rescued without upsetting this stellar equilibrium. But that was why she was created. So that the other Em could survive.

CHAPTER THIRTY-ONE

Em held Gaston's warm hand, lovingly squeezing his stubby, thick fingers as they strolled to a boulder near the edge of a cliff. They wore bottle-green two-piece tunics, courtesy of *Suppose We*'s depleting stores. The planet's new orbit took it closer to the sun but the air temperature had yet to stabilise. This orbit danced with wobbles only partly caused by the brown dwarf has-been sun. There were no ice sheets, but the seas had expanded, although less than Em would have thought. Perhaps the additional cloud cover from increased energy and turbulence had reflected back out to space more solar radiation than they used to receive. Time would tell. Meanwhile the familiar lowland mix of forest and grassland was spread like a quilt cover before her. Mostly pinks and sandy, with green swathes where rivers meandered. Em's nose filled with that petrichor earthy aroma after rain.

"Gas, not only do I worry about Penn, who won't get out of bed and makes no sense, but my other Em. Great that a kind of truce has been arranged but will she ever be allowed to return?"

"It is wonderful, *n'est ce pas*? Nature on Earth, now here."

Her hold on his hand tightened, hoping it would squeeze a proper answer out of him. His eyes shut for a moment, so she let him go.

While she sat on the white limestone boulder, Gaston stooped over it to examine a tiny orange flower. "I cannot sit here and obliterate this *petite fleur*. I must record it."

"Will she?"

"*Voila*, I will sit on this bit even though there will be microscopic life. One can only go so far to avoid harming life. What? Ah, Em. *Je suis désolé*, it will be most probable that she has already died."

Em's stomach knotted and her face heated as she hit him hard on the shoulder. "What? I wouldn't have agreed to the swap if she was definitely going to be killed!"

Gaston stood rubbing his left arm and his eyebrows steepled. "Not killed, just died, as did the other experimental Ems."

He stepped away before she could hit him again. She lunged but only to grab his hand just as his foot slipped over the edge of the cliff. Em yanked him harder such that they both fell on the lilac grass. She jumped up and pointed a finger while yelling at him.

"What d'you fucking mean about experimental Ems? Stop. Let me guess. You used my cloned genetic material on small mammals and the first died after a few minutes, the second after a day, the third—"

Gaston, still in the wet grass, groaned. "No, no, no. I'd never be a party to such barbaric use of our fellow creatures. She's AI, Em. Machine with clever plastics and synth gels. Apparently..." He sat up, excited. Eyes bright. "... none of the Keps we see are as natural as we assumed."

"What? They're androids? Ew."

"Their brains, organs and much else are natural, but there is a lot of synth gel. Intelligent connective tissue. Just imagine if we had body parts like that."

"The other Ems?"

"*Oui*, they fast-grew cortex tissue with your genotype cells but while the H. NewKep is doing very well, which reminds me, we must... *non*? Later then. The new Em brain had to have higher functional abilities. *Difficile* in a developmental time-frame so short. The Keps managed to construct a full scale Em alive and talking, but its brain malfunctioned after a few hours. So..."

Em glowered at him. "So this Em we've sent to the Recs is expected to fall apart in when… a day, week?"

Gaston stood and fiddled with the belt of his tunic trousers as if he'd not noticed it before. "Not possible to know, except that she possesses a self-destruct module if synaptic behaviour indicates her speech and actions would give her away as not-you."

Em couldn't prevent her eyes misting. Tears dribbled down her cheeks. "That poor girl." She waved a fist at Gaston. "Don't you tell me she isn't a person. She's real. She has intelligence. Damn it, you vegan hypocrite. You're always banging on about animals should be respected for their sentience. *She* has it too. Agreed?"

"Of course, undeniable, but that isn't…how do I say this? Why we wanted her instead of you."

Em folded her arms tightly, daring him to faux pas himself to oblivion. "Say it. You didn't think I could do the job anymore. What, too obsessed with water while she isn't?"

The awkward moment was interrupted by Papillon flying between them. It settled on Em's shoulder to her surprise, then over to Gaston and its usual resting place on his shoulder bag.

Em took in a deep shuddering breath to gather her strength and thoughts.

CHAPTER THIRTY-TWO

CAN's CANTAKEROUS report

No wonder I am as unstable as the butterflies that aren't. Not only are too many of my circuits dedicated to tracking the remaining humans in their physical and mental states, but now I have to interface with the Kep flitters, Keps, Recs, faux Rec, Kep flitters, Kep faux Rec flitters, emergent H-NewKep, *Suppose We*'s original AI and now Em2. When will it end? Not yet.

I have to report that Em2 has succeeded in bringing the Recs to a mutually assured destruction / non-destruction impasse. Hopefully, it will persist in perpetuity. Sadly, it requires Em2 to remain in their custody, but I'm working on that. Perhaps we can arrange a cycling of Em clones.

Speaking of Em, Kep1 reports an unexpected change in the real human's chemistry of which she might not be aware. A conversation is needed.

Penn continues to deteriorate with senescence brought on—it is hypothesised by Science Officer Gaston Poirer—by the Keps walking through him. The Keps dispute this. I estimate he has 2,59,211 heart beats left or, for the non-incremental thinkers, one sidereal Earth month. There is a different possible outcome, another conversation about which I need to have.

Urgent need to investigate H.NewKep. They are restless.

Signed CAN

Date: Earth January 10^{h} *3646 Kepler New 366 days*

CHAPTER THIRTY-THREE

A few days later, Em tried to keep her mouth open while clutching onto the sides of the seat in the converted pod tearing through tunnels and occasionally out in the open. She glanced over at Gaston. His mouth also gaped so that his teeth didn't shatter with the vibration.

The first part of their journey was the worst. The required speeds and changes in direction had been fed into the AI unit in advance, treating them to lurches and crooked flying through cuestas and ravines. Em would have marvelled at the views through the porthole a lot more if she wasn't in imminent danger of throwing up.

"Gas, I told you to make this damned thing go slower than last time."

"*Bien sur*, it is twenty percent slower," he gasped while his knuckles whitened from grabbing his harness. "It's beautiful out there *n'est ce pas*? The sky is a swirling dance of lilac—"

"My God, Gaston, your breath. You've found garlic on this planet? But you should have given some to me too." She wanted to pinch her nose but dared not release her grip on the straps.

"Allicin is an organo-sulphur compound, not difficult to create with *Suppose We*'s three-d food printer."

"Next time, print a mint."

Gaston laughed. "Tell me, Em, I think you had a discussion via CAN with Kep1 over Penn?"

She pulled a long face and recalled her heated exchange with Kep1 via CAN.

"Kep, could you have cloned Delta like you did with me?"

Kep had replied, "Of course."

"Then why didn't you?"

"You did not request it."

Em's tears burst out. "What? Wasn't it obvious? ...ugh!"

"I do not understand."

"Okay. Is it now too late to clone Delta?"

"No. If this is your wish, please give us some body material. However, it would be unlikely that the clone would be as successful as yours."

"How about Penn?"

"Commander Penn is in a condition unknown to us. We continue to monitor and offer assistance."

"Yes, thanks but I now assume you can clone him?"

"I do not believe that is his wish."

Em recalled going weak at the knees and having to sit. "Really? But he's not been able to talk coherently for days. Are you tapping into his mind?"

"I do not understand."

Em's mind misted.

⊙X⊙

Gaston hugged her. "Do not worry, *ma chérie,* we will sort it out."

He had no idea how they were going to save Penn. When his jealous side overtook reason, he was glad Penn was ill. Too incapacitated to make another play for Em, however, he wouldn't wish Penn to become a permanent vegetable or to die. On the other hand would he want a clone, fit, active and superior Penn#2, Penn#3,...Penn#n to be around?

Papillon fluttered its lilac wings in front of his face as if trying to attract his attention. Gaston hadn't told Em yet that the creature had been given to him by Kep1. A great honour for a human to 'possess' in an obscure way, a creature so beautiful, elegant and clumsy at the same time. A flying figment perhaps. *Oui*, Kep1 apparently could grow a new one and that Papillon had grown attached to this strange human. Gaston queried its purpose in life. He thought it wasn't independent but a symbiot perhaps taking sustenance from within Kep1 when it homed, so to speak. Kep1 didn't deny this. Merely that a small biological change allowed a human to 'adopt' Papillon. Then Kep1 intimated something bizarre, as if the gift was not strange enough.

The butterfly was sometimes here and not here. Not as Gaston thought with Quantum Entanglement or a kind of Schrödinger butterfly, but it could travel between dimensions. He would have laughed that notion out of the sand tray a year ago, but now, after all he'd seen lately?

While hurtling around in the pod, fielding complaints from Em, Gaston allowed his mind to wander. A while ago he'd asked Kep1, "How do you communicate with Papillon."

'As you do.'

"*Mais non.* I cannot speak butterfly!"

'How do you feel when you see it flying towards you?'

Gaston couldn't help smiling. "An intense glow of pleasure."

'It feels the same. It is the beginning of communication. Now it and you are one, you will find it develops exponentially.'

Gaston, in the pod, smiled at that last remark. The problem with exponential growth was that it could increase by nearly nothing for a long, long time. He only hoped the dramatic increase would happen before another year was out. He'd yet to inform Em about his symbiot, worried she might reject the two of them.

⊙ Ӿ ⊙

Back in the pod being hurled in half-tunnels, Em called out, "Gaston you're daydreaming. Watch out!"

The pod took a sharp left.

Em screamed than yelled, "I'm going to throw up. Hang on, that's the edge!"

Gaston talked faster than she'd ever heard him, but she wasn't taking in what he said. She saw he was punching the console. She too tried to override the auto-controls with the cliff-edge only moments away.

She held her breath, as if that would help. The pod didn't slow, it shot off horizontally before starting a descent, tilting forward giving her a view of a canyon floor a kilometre below. Ochre rocks and a meandering river waiting for them. Her mouth opened to release another scream but cognitive functions overrode the unnecessary noise.

She found she could speak but only in panic gasps. "Just a minute. Gas. This used to be...our escape pod. It could fly."

"*Exactement.* I've been looking into it."

Now she screamed just as her eyes widened at the rapidly approaching ground. "Just do it!"

"No fuel."

"What? How did we—"

"The tunnel propelled us. A mixture of magnetism, induction—"

"Never mind that. We're about to die!" Her stomach knotted and perspiration stung her eyes. "Is this the end?"

"Not yet, *ma chérie.* Ah, there it is."

The pod violently halted its downward acceleration. Her harness dug into her ribs but at least she wasn't meat paste on the ceiling.

"The chute! You knew all along, you bastard." Yet she laughed with relief.

"I wasn't sure that it had been stowed, or packed correctly. We're still in trouble. *Regardez!*" He pointed at the porthole. No matter how slowly they landed, it would be into a raging torrent. Even from over two-hundred metres up, she saw sharp rocks jutting above the white water.

"Lose ballast," she shouted.

"Let me see," Gaston muttered, as he hovered fingertips over the console.

"We've no time to search inventories. I'm losing the retros, fuel tanks, LSS—oh, it's not external. What's this BSeg? It's external. It's going."

"No!" Gaston threw his hand over hers, but too late. "It is the base segment of this pod. Now we won't need a porthole."

Em's face heated with embarrassment as through her

dangling feet she saw the curved floor descend faster than themselves.

Gaston shook his head. "Now, when we crash into that river—"

"Yes, I get it."

"Not only that, Em, but the alloy for that segment weighed less than my leg. It's not—"

"I get that, too. Enough. Oh, God." Her stomach knotted and tears filled her eyes at the thought of them being torn to pieces while inside the pod that should've protected them for a few seconds. She gripped her harness as if it would help then realized they might not get wet or smashed. "We've slowed, haven't we?"

"*Oui*. The parachute has deployed and is billowing. There, we have stopped falling, but, but..."

Em relaxed her unnecessary grip on her harness and muttered, "Oh no, not falling up again. This time it's the chute, isn't it?"

"I do not believe we're in a gravity anomaly here, Em, although they are unstable, drifting."

Em flicked fingers over the console. "I don't suppose we possess a working gravimeter, I can't keep dropping my beaker to see if it's falling faster, or not at all. Plus, there's a good chance it'd fall out of the pod and it's my last."

Gaston laughed as if relieved they weren't falling although Em realised he could find her rant amusing. "Em, we're rising from the parachute catching an updraft, possibly an anabatic lift from the meeting of katabatics in the centre of the valley. No gravity anomaly."

"How can you be so sure?"

Gaston coughed—one of his I'm-embarrassed noises rather than his usual wheezing. "Papillon told me."

"Come again?"

"Kep gave me the creature. Did you know?"

"All I know, Gas, is that we're about to collide with that cliff face. Should we try and swing the pod?"

He laughed again and shook his head. "We've lost what

manoeuvring was engineered into this craft. Most parachutes can be steered but not this one. Just wait, *ma chérie.*"

"I must say, Gas, your jokiness confuses me. We could be dashed to death at any—what the hell?"

A noise like wind blowing through trees filled the pod, which drifted away from the cliff, and downwards.

"Is it your anabatic wind, Gas? If so, in spite of the din it's weakening and taking us for a drink among those boulders in the ravine."

Damn, if Gaston didn't stop grinning soon she'd belt him, hard.

"Watch. We are perfectly safe. We're being taken to a H-NewKep site of interest down there, and—"

"Being taken? By whom?"

"Papillon and its friends, the real butterflies. As big as plates. *Regardez.*"

Relieved they'd moved from the cliff, Em's head was, nevertheless, becoming cotton wool. Confusion, still in danger, odd input, and a dark cloud of butterflies taking the parachute and hence them gently downwards.

"The butterfly is *yours*? Explain."

"It's a personal entity, symbiotically related to its host, which was Kep1, but now given to me. Please don't ask too much, I'm a novice and learning."

CHAPTER THIRTY-FOUR

Gaston jumped out of the pod, which had come to rest two metres above a mass of purple vegetation the Frenchman hoped wasn't brambles.

Em called, "Is it all right for me to jump now?"

Gaston couldn't answer immediately because in an effort to disengage from the nebulous and adhesive bush. He'd turned upside down with his head inside its cavernous interior. He saw spiders and once again wondered what they ate if they weren't predators. Could they be eating this tacky slime, or excreting it. Ugh, *merde*. His nostrils pinched with the sour odour of old yoghurt but with a hint of vanilla. He ought to keep a sample. At least it was cooler in there as opposed to the body-temperature ambience outside. A flashback of a childhood hike in the woods where he became tangled in bindweed worried him. After a few moments of struggling, he twisted round so while immersed in the tangle, he could see upwards.

"*Un moment*, nothing sharp sticking into me but these willowy stems and leaves are sticking to my suit, impeding my... ah, I understand why Papillon's friends didn't place the pod down here." He was afraid the amorphous, thornless brier was aggressive as an inquisitive, or ravenous animal. His right arm itched as if to remind him of the cucumber tree that ate through it.

"Gas, the pod's twisting round. Erm, I think you should've waited a few minutes 'cos there's dry land over there."

The pod rotated so the hatch and Em turned out of sight. Then to Gaston's squirming horror, it started to descend with excruciating slowness right on top of him.

Ironically, Em's mistake of ejecting the base panel while in flight, saved him from being pushed deeper, suffocating, into the plant. He grabbed a seat harness and with great difficulty hauled himself up and into the pod. He glanced back at the frustrated foliage, distinctly sagging in despondency.

He despaired at the slime sticking to his green coveralls, but had no means in the pod to clean it off, so he stumbled to the hatch and jumped the remaining metre to dry ground and followed Em around a boulder. His despondency from a feeling the planet was fighting him in the last hour dissipated when he saw a white figure.

"Kep! *Mon vieux*, how did you get here so quickly?"

His answer came via Gaston's earpiece. 'Question one: why you are so slow? Humans still use conveyances. Question two: Do you enjoy your glueness?'

"No, but I have no means at hand to clean it off."

'You do.'

Kep1 bent backwards as if he was looking upwards.

Gaston's eyes followed and he saw the cloud of butterflies.

"I do not know how to control *those*!"

'You do.'

He spotted Papillon leaving the others and zigzagging towards him. *D'accord.* He couldn't give commands because that wasn't the way. He looked at his hands and clothes. "Papillon, *mon ami*, I am all sticky and wish to be—"

Once again a shimmering mass descended slowly upon him, and he trembled with the unknown. Before he had time to perspire more, his vision blurred with all the rainbow colours—and some—on this strange planet. A drunken vision of wings coloured pinks, greens, rich blues, purples and supernumerary hues that appeared fluorescent. He tried to focus on one but it was replaced like a kaleidoscope of butterflies. He mind-swirled with them in a frenetic elation.

His eyes squeezed shut wanting this moment to stretch

for... then their soft pressure lifted. Seeing, once again, Papillon fluttered to his shoulder bag. Gaston poked at his green tunic. The stickiness had gone.

"Did you see that, Em?"

"Of course. It was amazing!"

"But did you observe what they were doing? Too dark for me."

Em laughed at him and ran a hand up his sleeve and over his face.

"You've found your own dry cleaners!"

CAN burst into their ears. 'Advisable to concentrate on the mission today. The H.NewKep is getting out of hand. Go to Kep1 immediately. It will mean much more to you to see for yourself.'

"Okay, CAN," Em said, "keep your knickers on."

Gaston released a short guffaw but headed towards a swamp area where their Kep hovered.

From the pod, Em brought a sampling kit. "Hey, Gas, how are we going to get to Kep1? I've not brought waders and no way am I exposing my flesh in those murky waters. Remember those eels a few months back?"

"*Oui*, sometimes I think our hosts forget we walk on the ground. Let's see."

Em walked besides him along the muddy tract with the human-grabbing shrubbery on the right and swamp on the left, reeking of bad eggs. She released a cry when her left leg sank in up to her knee. Gaston put his arm around her shoulder to lift her, then let go.

"*Regardez*, this mud isn't all mud!"

"I don't care what it is, help me out of it. Ugh, it's—they're wriggling up my thigh! Gaston, you bastard, get me up and get that stuff off me."

He knelt in the soft mud and scooped a handful of the tiny puce creatures off her thigh. "*C'est incredible*, like miniature shell-less turtles. See, a bulbous middle, stubby, cute tail. Two black pupils. Specimen jar quick as you please."

She rummaged in the satchel. "You sure they're not harmful? They're slimy but might have teeth."

"No, no I cannot be sure of anything until we study." He looked up at Kep1. "Are they a Kepler 20h species?"

CAN interrupted. 'We doubt it. Evidence so far, suggests it is a rapidly-evolving H.NewKep.'

"*C'est absurd*, that should be a mere group of cells, bacteria...so this is why you sent those concerned, panicky memoranda?"

CAN streamed random digits into Gaston's head, followed by, 'I do not panic. My reports were measured and considered—'

Em interrupted the AI with a quote: "Oh dear, oh dear, oh dear, oh dear, oh dear. Recall that one, CAN?"

'Had I transmitted tha—so I did. Apologies. A slip of a node. Getting back to what is important for life and its future on this planet, please take samples back to the base.'

"As long as you do not expect me to dissect them alive. Ah, you know it is not necessary with the Kep scanning equipment."

Em, recovered, held two of the thumbnail-sized creatures in the palm of her hand. "Cutting them is a no-no, but are they amphibious? I can't see any in the water but if I place my hand at surface layer... look there they go. Hah, like tiny terrapins. Well, Gaston, are they vegan, or carnivores as on Earth?"

"Good point, being a new hybrid species, it will be interesting to observe their habits. Terran green sea turtles are herbivores."

Em scooped up another one crawling up inside her tunic trousers. "We didn't plant Earth turtle DNA, but human, and apart from a minority, homo sapiens are omnivorous. Yes?" She let the creature scuttle onto a leaf.

Gaston studied a group of the amphibians. "Complicated, *ma chérie*, we've evolved into a more ethical phase, so even if our systems can digest garbage, we can choose not to."

He took a few steps closer to Kep1. "Ah, there are different coloured ones over here. Yellows, pinks, speckled. Pity they are so odorous."

Kep1 shook as if agitated. Gaston had trouble again with his own ear translator. Luckily, CAN was listening in.

'Kep1 is agitated over the H.NewKep and their exponential increase in size and number. So am I.'

Gaston smiled at Kep1. "All flora and fauna have exponential growth as they grow, although to be honest, I anticipated this would stay as a bacterial form for many years. Why, exactly, are you both worried?"

CAN returned immediately, 'It is what you, on Earth, would call an invasive species. It appears to be successfully adapting to the planetary ecosystem perhaps too well.'

"You mean to the exclusion of other species, but are they forcing them out of their habitats?"

'No. Not the point.'

"*S'il vous plaît*, then what is your point?"

'The need for control. You do not know how they are developing, the extent of their habitation, nor their long-term effects on the ecosystem.'

Em stamped her feet but stopped when it made a squelching rather than a stomping noise and the horrible thought of squishing lifeforms. "Just a freaking minute, Kep. Have you forgotten why the human DNA-engineered bacteria was distributed by your flitters as far as possible? We were doing this planet a favour."

After a few moments, CAN communicated with, 'While the natives are grateful for being rid of the harmful bacteria, Humanity benefitted too. Also, you speculated that the new bacterium would take millions of years to develop limbs and intelligence.'

Gaston bent over to examine their feet. "I hope, Em, you didn't crush any of the H.NewKeps when you danced just then."

"So do I. Gas we can't keep calling them by their taxonomy label."

After he'd stooped down, one crawled into his open hand. "What do you suggest?"

"Peeps. I had a pet turtle called Peeps and these little critters remind me of her."

"Umm, isn't it slang for People? But then the Keps won't know that and perhaps not, CAN."

'I can hear you.'

Em put her hand to her mouth. "We've forgotten to switch

him off. Oh well. What do you think of Peeps for the H.NewKep, CAN?"

'Poops would be more accurate considering their excrement in which you are standing. For me, you can call them 101010 for all I care. A moment. Feedback from the Keps. They would rather their name—the Kep you call them—be incorporated. Perhaps Keeps? Back to the problem though. It might be possible to tag their distribution. Is that not so?'

Gaston continued to examine the one in a tiny puddle on his palm. "It's hard to think of these miniature naked turtles as in any way human. They will, no doubt, continue to change."

Em prodded his elbow. "Keeps is fine by me. After all, they are keepers of our line and were born on a Kep planet. Answer CAN, will you, before you drift off again."

Gaston put a thoughtful finger on his lips, then removed it when he recalled that he'd touched a keep with it. "Biometric signatures can be picked up for any species at close range. I'm uncertain whether these H...keeps are sufficiently bulked to emit such a signal. Have the flitters been equipped with receivers and tested?"

'They are advanced in those preparations and possess your specifications for the DNA segmentation, but need your input on more details.'

Gaston grinned at Em. "Hear that, Em, a species a million years ahead of us need my help. Ha! *D'accord*. I'll come right away."

Em put her hand on his chest. "No you won't, lover boy."

Gaston's eyebrows steepled.

"Conditions. They need your brains, we need theirs. Make them help Penn. With cloning or whatever to undo what they did to him."

Gaston stuck out his lower lip, then, "Hmm, they indicate that they didn't see us – so to speak – when they walked through Delta and Penn at that time, and even if they did, they remain unsure what biological changes have happened. However, if they cannot reverse his senescence, they do have the means to clone him. And try to create another Delta."

Em brought a turtle in her palm up to eye level. "This is

rather weird, young keep. Besides the original population, this world might soon be populated by two ordinary humans, two or more cloned humans, who might or might not be like they were when on Earth, and you guys. How friendly are we all going to be?”

CHAPTER THIRTY-FIVE

Em sat on the edge of a limestone ridge overlooking a wide forested plain to pale mauve hills on the horizon. One of the nearby shrubs emitted a jasmine-like fragrance bringing her a temporary smile. Angst knotted her stomach which might dissipate when she told Gaston, or it would intensify.

The sky assumed a painter's palette, but mostly pinks, and hues of whole damn bunches of roses. It could be a sunset from the west coast of Ireland where her Grannie lived. Sunset here too. She recalled one of the folk weather lore:

"Red sky at night, shepherd's delight. Gas, do you think that was true on Earth?"

Sat besides her, he was pouring an amber liquid into two beakers looking like they were cut from bamboo stalks. He sipped one and grinned. "You will enjoy this, lager girl." She took it from him and set it down. "*Oui*, that saying is about seventy percent true on Earth according to a Prévisions Meteo France report but here on Kepler-20h, who knows? Too many reds in the sky. However, *that* is of more interest." He pointed at the horizon directly west, in front of them.

The normally bright ballet-slipper pink sun had turned green. "On Earth, *ma cherie*, that is known as a green flash and lasts up to two seconds. Here, much longer. You are thinking why green, no?"

"No. You've told me a dozen times. The blues of shorter wavelengths refract and scatter out to space while the longer reds and yellows are absorbed. Leaving green to be visible. Never mind the science, it's just beautiful."

"*Oui,* it takes longer here because this planet rotates more slowly, giving us longer—"

She'd put a finger to his lips. He kissed it.

"Let's just absorb the moment, Gaston. Peace. The Recs are holding off indefinitely, Penn is drifting off in himself while Delta is being recreated. See, Papillon is doing a happy dance."

"Indeed, and the keeps are as contented as new babies can be. Try your new elixir." He picked hers up, tempting her to sample its sweet aroma.

She sniffed and her tongue dipped into the drink. "It's one of your alcoholic experiments, isn't it? A cocktail, no doubt a mere variety of formaldehyde." She laughed at his mock hurt face.

"You're normally eager to quaff my concoctions. Anyone would think... *quoi, vraiment?* A baby?" His eyebrows disappeared into his ragged black hair and she'd never seen his smile so broad. Um, one of his teeth might need looking at. He stopped grinning for a moment to blurt, "But, that is wonderful. Allow me."

He emptied both their drinks over the edge of the cliff. Papillon flew after them as if it wanted to taste a drop.

Gaston shuffled closer and put an arm around her. "Just imagine...think of it. Our future life with a little one. He or she will grow up on this odd but quaint planet, learning so much. I can't wait to tell someone! Penn had better wake up, and Delta created. Papillon, Kep1, CAN. We'll tell the world. Em, this is so...why are you...are those tears of happiness?"

Between sobs she nodded but also shook her head. "I want all that to be true, Gas, but—but just suppose the baby is...and I've not been able to test this though Kep1 has been working on it. I only know I'm pregnant because of a missed period."

"There were pregnancy test kits on *Suppose We*, I presume..."

"Yes, yes, of course, but you're missing..."

His mouth gaped and he stood, knocking over the flask of drink. He took a few steps back.

"Careful, Gaston, we're on the edge of a cuesta and there are rocks."

He turned and walked a few steps holding his head in his hands. She told herself it was shock. He wasn't rejecting her, or, hopefully not the child, even if a hybrid could be called such. She stood in case he got too near the edge again.

He returned and cautiously put an arm around her. "You've not been pregnant before, so it's not you feeling different this time, and no blood or urine, or other tests yet? You...and Penn?"

She kept silent for a few minutes. "It's not Penn's. I've not even kissed him like we do. CAN says there are some biochemical irregularities that don't match anything in its medical databases. Do you hate me?"

His silence was worse, she thought.

"Of course not. I will always love you. Do you really think that when that Kep...what was its name?"

"Uooueuz with some identifiers, HX and C."

He paced around. "You believe it impregnated you? Or..."

"Or what? Ah, are you thinking that it was you, but that somehow your wrigglies, or my ovum, have been contaminated? I'd not thought of that."

Gaston shook his head. "I'm clutching at straws, but it would be wise to check it out. Has CAN checked?"

Its voice came through both of their implants. 'It has the signature of Keplerian as well as human male and female reproduction cells. All three of you."

Em lifted her tunic top and stroked her stomach even though nothing showed. "A tri-fertilized, cross-species being. Another first, eh, Gaston?"

He walked over and placed his hand on hers. "I will love our, your...*d'accord*, our offspring, whatever or whoever it is."

Watch this space for book three!

Not literally watch this space although with the pace of technology, who knows? By the time ***Son of Kepler*** is ready, it could appear in this space.

Geoff Nelder

Geoff Nelder has a wife, two grown-up kids, and a handful of lively grandchildren. He lives in rural England within an easy cycle ride of the Welsh mountains.

Publications include several non-fiction books on climate reflecting his other persona as a Fellow of the Royal Meteorological Society; over 90 published short stories in various magazines and anthologies; thriller, humour, science fiction, and fantasy novels. He's been a fiction judge on several occasions, and has co-written a guide on winning short story competitions.

Social Media and other links for Geoff Nelder

Twitter @geoffnelder
Facebook https://www.facebook.com/geoffnelder
Facebook page for ARIA Trilogy
https://www.facebook.com/AriaTrilogy
Facebook page for XAGHRA'S REVENGE
https://www.facebook.com/xaghrasrevenge
Science fiction database http://www.sf-encyclopedia.com/entry/nelder_geoff
LinkedIn https://www.linkedin.com/in/geoff-nelder-39170a3/
Website https://geoffnelder.com

Incremental

Geoff's stunning collection of sci-fi, speculative, and bizarre fiction!

Excerpts that will whet your appetite...

View From...

At last I open my eyes... and I discover that *I am on the ceiling*.

I laugh. Nerves. Then my stomach knots. I *am* on the ceiling, looking down. Has Alan re-arranged my room during sleeptime in order to make it appear inverted?

I squeeze my eyelids shut then slowly re-open them. Below, covered with an untidy red quilt, is my bed. The bed-side cabinet is next to it, supporting the alarm clock, which periodically bursts into indignation at being ignored.

I send my impending terror into an unused corner of brain, a trick learnt when teaching difficult classes.

Has a trickster stuck my furniture down? My right arm that had swung into action has returned up to the ceiling. Turning my head, I see the white ceiling-rose. I've not seen my Georgian ceiling this close up. Cracks in the paintwork and plaster missing near the rose tell me that I should get workmen in. Banality subjugates fear.

Gravity's Tears

Emma clamped her hands to her ears as the pickup

started a forward roll amidst an ear-hurting metallic screaming. The cacophony increased as her arm was yanked by Quill, pulling her out of the way of the oncoming disaster. The stench of burning rubber and spilling gas assaulted her nose as the cartwheeling pickup hurtled inches from her. Wooden crates floated in the air, travelling with the rear of the pickup. Something hard bashed Emma's left arm as Quill continued pulling her to the verge. She closed her eyes yearning for the bad-movie to finish. She'll open them when *The End* flashed up.

"Stay here," Quill said.

A thump on the trailer's roof grabbed her attention for a fraction before gasping in horror at the pickup now upside down, and about to crash onto their Dodge. The adrenaline buzz slowed her perception of time. Tensing her muscles for a potential explosion, her heart raced. She could see the pale shirtsleeve of the driver. Tears smeared her vision as she imagined his helplessness as the collision continued. Through the horror she had to admire the solid construction of both vehicles. Although a tyre exploded on the Dodge, as it skidded sideways, neither roof collapsed.

"He needs to get outta there," Quill said. "Spilt gas everywhere, all those sparks."

"No sparks now."

"Our engine's still running. I should go help him."

"No—if you think it'll blow, then—hey, did you hear that?" Up the road another detonation. Meteorites. Had she read that article wrong? It said the shooting stars didn't reach the ground. Quill stepped towards the crashed cars. Emma grabbed his elbow. In pain they both uttered gasps.

"Bummer, what's that?" He held out his arm to show a tear in his black leather jacket sleeve. Raspberry oozed out. Her nose caught a whiff of charred fabric and her eyes took in the seeping gash, spoiling a dagger tattoo. Then downwards to a wisp of smoke from the grass between them.

"Must've been debris from the pickup, or one of your meteorites," he said. Silently, she turned her attention to her own left arm. Just a bruise.

"I can't *not* help him." Quill pulled from her but stopped as another projectile slammed into the pickup's upside-down base sending both vehicles shaking. Another hit the road beside Emma. She pulled Quill around to look at a saucer-sized crater in the tarmac, and then the corona of another formed as they watched. Percussions hammered around them.

466Hz

As Robert alighted a high note rang through his head. He couldn't source it, not even the approximate direction. What was the point of having two ears if he couldn't use them stereoscopically to locate a noise? He stood at the now empty plexiglass bus stop with its rolling advert of what scantily-clad people look like with Vit K Oil. He tilted his head up and decided the noise was a pure tone, B-flat above middle C. All that piano practise as a teen.

A dog howled as if it heard the noise too.

No doubt the sound was a decelerating jet bringing another 180 Brits to Palma airport.

If the lane he walked down hadn't have been closed to traffic he wouldn't have noticed the persistence of the whining noise. The lane meandered through the Maquis vegetation, emitting wafts of lavender. He couldn't spot wires that might have vibrated. A goat bleated. They've always liked his kind of alien.

Could goats hear it?

The terracotta-coloured block peeped over its Bougainvillea shrubbery. Robert stopped at the marbled entrance to listen again. The noise persisted. He needed to ask someone else. Señora Gimenez waddled up the pavement loaded with shopping. No point asking her. Too late, she was talking to him.

"Señor Smith, do you hear it too?"

"Indeed, I do, Marta. Annoying isn't it? Can I help you up the stairs with your bags?"

She let him take the overstretched bags. "I hear it this morning in the supermercado."

He lifted her bags. "You did? I only heard it an hour ago. Did everyone hear it?"

"Oh yes. We're all annoyed they're closing the post office. It's not good, is it?"

He carried Marta's bags to her ground floor flat, returned her smile, and trudged up the stairs to his apartment. His BOSE SoundDock poised ready to blast Pink Floyd around his room but instead, Robert relaxed into his yellow vinyl armchair and listened.

It was there. A single note and it penetrated into the room even with the windows closed. He booted up his PC, made himself a coffee, plonked himself on his swivel chair, triggered Audacity and recorded a minute of what should have been near silence.

The display, looking like a heart monitor told him the sound was real. 466 Hertz at 39 decibels. B-flat, easily heard by any human including Marta. He attached a microphone and took it to a window he'd just opened. To his surprise the sound level remained at 39 dB. Well, his gear was good for an amateur but only just. He wondered again if the phenomenon was local, a factory testing engines.

Time to go worldwide. He'd start with the nearest city, Palma. Any odd noises reported on the web? There, a noise heard so persistent they had to close the restaurant until the Health Department checked it out. Robert frowned. There was no Health Department as such on the island. Ah, it was the Palma Restaurant, NYC. Just a minute. If New York was hearing the same noise...

LOCKED OUT

Out of the airlock I spin slowly to take in the magnificent view of the comet's tail, like champagne bursting out of its magnum although with a fluttering of incandescent colours difficult to define. Monet's palette with a splattering of effervescent turquoise and virgin's blush. That comet was identified as a simple asteroid 93 years ago in 2006 then it flared, altered course a smidgen and is expected to slam into Mercury at 1803 tomorrow.

The Mercury planet that is only a thousand kilometres away. I rotate more and there's the sun with its angular size four times larger than from Earth. I'm not melting, not in this suit.

Mars is so yesterday. Our surveillance craft, *Snowy Owl*, bristles with instruments yet the most important, our communications with Earth is out.

Hand over hand I reach the high-gain antenna. It's not working, especially when we're dodging about and it's attempting to aim at Houston. Problem is that the low-gain is twitchy too.

Our *Snowy Owl* looks like layers of an onion, designed to keep us cool and shielded inside. Comfy, yet she's in there and I'm out in the hard radiation, fiddling.

How many Earthbound would consider using a screwdriver and pliers while wearing their Aunty Joan's thickest gardening gloves?

The wrench won't turn. It needs to rotate the bolt anticlockwise, otherwise the high-gain antennae housing will stay shut forever, malfunctioning. I'm in danger of puncturing my glove if I push too hard. Need more leverage so I fetch up my faithful rubber mallet and play tap along. "Why are you being so stubborn? Come along, bolt, be nice to Uncle Kiu."

Static fills my helmet. "Kiu, who are you talking to, over?" Her intonation carries a southern drawl, unhurried, purring, annoying.

"Hello, Suzi, good to hear a calming voice. I've temporarily imbued a component of the antenna with emotion so it will respond to friendly persuasion."

"Idiot. It's stuck, then?"

I tap the Allen key end again but it's not moving. "I'm afraid so, please shut your ears when my urging gives way to cursing."

In a warm workshop back in Idaho I'd be able to squirt WD-40 onto a seized bolt. Out here, liquid tends to become micro-droplets in the near vacuum and spread everywhere except where it's wanted. Even so there are other DIY tricks.

I rotate my utility belt and reach for an exothermal pad. I pull apart a top layer and stick the base around the bolt. In moments it heats up by thirty degrees. The expansion followed quickly by contraction might loosen the stubborn metal lump.

"I'm still here, Suzi. I'm trying a bit of thermal trickery."

"What the hell? D'you know how thin this skin is?"

Umm, her language dialect module requires adjustment. She goes overboard sometimes, not literally from a spaceship although that's where I am. Ah, the trick works and I turn the Allen key.

She's talking at me again. "All that fuss just to remove one pokey panel. Now stow the tools before extracting and using the voltmeter on—"

"Hey, Suzi, I've got this. Sing me a song. You know I love your Dolly Parton impressions."

"Go boil your head, Kui."

There's distortion in the panel as if the heat-pad melted the circuit board. "That's not down to me. Something else is going on here... overload or under-insulation. No matter, I can reconstruct this board with spares. I'm coming in." I'm certain the exothermal heat-pad isn't responsible for the damage. Sabotage? Did Suzi do this?

Hatches can be operated with smart actuators but I like the simple approach. Lift the handle, twist and pull. A built-in resistance, then I'm inside the airlock. Usually. The handle wouldn't twist. It should turn anticlockwise to unlock but it's as stubborn as the bolt. Is seizing-up becoming infectious on this mission?

"Hey, Suzi, the hatch won't open manually, I'm going for electronic command and if that fails I'll ask you to kindly open the door."

I try audio commands. Nothing. I open an outer flap on my sleeve and jab at the keypad. "Suzi, nothing's working. Let me in please."

In the silence that follows, my face heats up. Maybe with the stress of the uncertain situation or my suit's homeostasis is malfunctioning.

I extract my divers' message whiteboard and scribble, 'Plse Opn Htch!' and wave it at two of the cams.

No reaction.

"Suzi, are you okay? I'm sorry for that quip yesterday about the pimple on your left cheek. It's hardly noticeable. Ah, I've made things worse. Let me in, Suzi. It's lonely out here. Nearest neighbour is over forty million miles away and I can't converse with them cos of the antenna... Suzi?"

I extract a wrench and...

...knock on the door. Three taps, pause tap, pause tap, pause tap then three more taps.

"Come on, Suzi, even if your radio and cams aren't working you must hear my S.O.S. Have a heart."

Nothing.

I could knock harder but it isn't a steel hatch. Polycarbonate and aluminium alloy dents easily. She'll worry if I keep banging, so I do, and accompany it with fresh urging.

"Suzi, I have more tools. In fact there's a way in I've just thought of that is available to me and my tool belt if I—whoa, don't rock the boat!"

The spacecraft lurches away as she fires a burst of hydrazine at me.

"No, Suzi, you forget I'm tethered, you can't shake me off." She could if she throws me off with more than the 200 Newtons force warranty on this tether.

She's locked me out. I have sixteen minutes to get inside.

CHICKEN

I can't decide which is worse, the tandem harness hugging me too tightly to my suicidal friend, or how to yell above the wind that I've changed my mind.

Printed in Great Britain
by Amazon